SEVEN SIDES OF SELF

SEVEN
SIDES
OF SELF

STORIES

· · · · · · · · · · · ·

NANCY JOIE WILKIE

SHE WRITES PRESS

Published November 5, 2019
Printed in the United States of America
Print ISBN: 978-1-63152-634-3
E-ISBN: 978-1-63152-635-0
Library of Congress Control Number: 2019907666

For information, address:
She Writes Press
1569 Solano Ave #546
Berkeley, CA 94707

Cover and interior design by Tabitha Lahr

She Writes Press is a division of SparkPoint Studio, LLC.

*This collection of short stories is
dedicated to all of those who have encouraged me
to pursue my writing, my music, and my art.
Special thanks to Jennifer, Amy, John, Beyhan,
Jim and Barb, and my editor, Rebecca.
And—oh, yes—to my Dad.*

CONTENTS

PREFACE

· · · · · · · · · · · ·

IT ALL CAME TO ME in a flash. I had just spent the morning exploring my favorite art museum. My mind was full of ideas for new art pieces and projects. I then made the short drive to the nearby artisan village. After visiting several shops, I found myself hungry and walked over to a little sundry shop—simply yummy. I placed my order and prepared myself for a wait of a dozen minutes.

Without warning, the idea for this collection of stories came to me. By the time my sandwich and salad arrived, I had sketched out the general structure for the book on a paper napkin. As I stepped back out into the hot southern afternoon after finishing lunch, I carried with me the seeds for *Seven Sides of Self* firmly registered in my mind.

Oh, yes—and I had a beaming smile on my face! The Muses had chosen to bless me once again with their spark and inspiration. GOD bless them!

July 28, 2010

THERE ONCE WAS A MAN . . .

(The Storyteller)

. . . .

THERE ONCE WAS A MAN who wanted to write. He wasn't quite sure why he wanted to write. He wasn't even sure about what to write. He only knew he felt a strong urge to write and that was all there was to it. He had always envied the great wordsmiths, their seemingly boundless pools of creativity, and the ease with which their words flowed across vast numbers of pages. He was fascinated by the ability of his favorite authors to paint grand vistas and draw people into imaginary journeys with just the right sequence of words.

He surprised himself during his first years of college by actually putting some of his thoughts onto paper. In his spare time, he managed to collect a notebook full of poetry and even wrote a short story. His early attempts at writing pleased him. Then graduation came along and a full-time job filled up his life. Just as many aspiring professionals often do, he focused on his career and put everything else on the back burner. So—despite his deep yearning to write—he devoted little time to writing in the years following college.

The older he got, the harder it seemed for him to sit down and write something. But he did still think about writing. When he turned thirty-five years old, he began to worry maybe he was too old and it was too late to start putting pen to paper. When he looked back at what he wrote fifteen years earlier, he feared what others might think of his creations. He feared his ideas would not be good enough and that no publisher would actually pay him for his work. He became convinced his efforts would never gain the respect and the admiration of others. More than anything, though, he dreaded discovering he had no true talent for writing.

"What if people think what I write is total gobbledy-gook?" he would muse. His father's age-old warnings would always break into his consciousness at this point in the man's internal struggle. "You can never make a living at writing! You need a respectable profession! You will have a family to feed!" Then the imposing voice of his mother would follow. "Stop daydreaming! You should be outside playing with the other boys instead of sitting in here and thinking about writing books!"

The need to resolve the creative yearnings of his heart with the voices inside his responsible and professional mind eventually came to a climax. The words "desire, ask, believe, and receive" jumped off the pages of a self-help book he read and filled his entire being with promise. He mulled over this sequence of words and their significance. Clearly, he had the desire. Maybe he had just never asked. But ask who? GOD?

And what about faith? Did he believe somewhere out in the Universe a Supreme Deity would provide the words if he just asked? More importantly, could he learn to resist the urge to judge himself and his creations too harshly if he did ask and did receive?

When he finally started to think seriously about what he could do to attain his long-dormant dream, he decided he would need to conquer his internal doomsayer. To silence this overbearing critic, he must overcome the self-doubt and start to think of himself as someone who could write and write well. To reinforce this idea, he decided that every morning when he awoke and every evening before he went to bed he would repeat to himself these words: "I am a writer. I am a good writer. The words I write are gifts given to me by the Creator. My role is to write the words, not to judge them."

At first, this exercise proved to be a very difficult thing to do. Something way down inside of him could not accept this mantra. With each passing day, the struggle to embrace the message lessened bit by bit. *Maybe the "someone inside" not wanting me to write is slowly giving up some of his claim over me,* he thought. *I need to rid myself of this shadow's hold on my dream.*

He also took a look at the many "someones outside"— those in his professional life and in his personal life. Did these people understand his need to be creative? Would they support his efforts to be creative? Or would they express unhappiness when they realized his writing took time and energy away from them?

This caused the man to consider another barrier to his goal—time. He came to the realization that unless he made a significant change in his lifestyle, there would never be time to write. He knew his job kept him very busy, and when not at work, household chores ate up his few free hours at night and on the weekends. So he made a commitment to himself to schedule time to write. The more he contemplated what it would require to reach his goal, the more he realized the size of the commitment he must make. When he first started to change his routine, he felt as though he must accomplish his dream in one giant step. As the months went by, he found taking a series of small steps to be more realistic, and he felt a sense of satisfaction with each baby step he took.

He next considered what other steps he might take to enhance his creative abilities. He decided he should surround himself with an environment that would stimulate his imagination. He resolved to build himself an office. No—better yet—a studio. And instead of the stark, barren walls in his extra bedroom, he would decorate his studio with posters and pottery. He would fill the room with comfortable furniture and a warm-colored rug. He would install stereo speakers so the retreat would reverberate with his favorite music. He could hardly wait!

Every spare hour during the next winter, the man spent planning, purchasing, building, and painting. At the end of each weekend, he would sit in his new room and relish each new accomplishment. He would imagine what the room would be like when finished. Before he knew it, the finishing touches to his new space were done.

"Today I will write!" he declared one sunny spring afternoon. "My new studio is complete, all of my errands are done, and all of the bills are paid. I no longer have any excuse not to finally start writing." He selected his favorite music and turned on his stereo. He felt the call of his idle typewriter and sat down in front of it.

"What shall I write about?" the man asked himself. He took several deep breaths. He let his mind wander. The minutes ticked by. After a while, he quietly remarked, "I've sat here for an hour and I don't know what to write about. In all of the years of wanting to write, I have only ever had glimpses of stories in my imagination. Now, I can't seem to capture anything on paper."

Another hour came and went and still the man had no inspiration. He felt as though he was a lumberjack who had finally sharpened his axe, ventured out into the forest, and arrived to find all of the trees chopped down with only stumps remaining. *Perhaps I will try again tomorrow*, he thought with a sigh.

The following morning the man again sat down at his desk. He opened up his mind, hoping for a spark to ignite some hidden story. One hour passed. A second hour passed. The man still was unable to put so much as a single word on paper.

The man then thought about the affirmations he had been repeating twice a day. He knew doing this exercise helped him to think of himself as a writer—or at least that someday he would be a writer. After all, it had helped him to create a writing space, and it had given him time in front of his typewriter. He found he did like the feel of walking into his studio and sitting down to write. Maybe that was it. But he now needed to start acting like a writer, too. If nothing else, he thought he would go into his new studio and sit at his desk while he recited his affirmations.

And even though no story, manuscript, or essay came to him, the process of going through the motions did make him feel better. As he sat in his antique desk chair one morning, a seemingly brilliant idea came to him.

"Maybe if I tried a different set of surroundings," said the man. "I need some fresh insight. Maybe some time away from my home would help to feed my starved imagination." With it being Saturday, the man got into his car and drove to a nearby scenic overlook. He studied the valley beneath him. He pondered the mountains around him. He listened to the cries of the birds. He smelled the sweet aroma of the flowers.

"If only I could describe the lushness of the vegetation in the valley or the majesty of the peaks, or put into words the awe I feel when I watch the circling of the birds overhead or smell the perfume of the flowers—and then could weave all of them into some spellbinding story," he mused. After several hours of surrounding himself with nature's richness without any stirring of his creative juices, he turned his car around and headed for home. He began to feel as though nothing would help him out of his predicament.

This pattern repeated itself many times over the following weeks and months. The man tried writing at different times and in different places. He tried reading books, watching movies, and visiting art museums—all with the hope something might unleash the spark he knew must be buried inside.

He asked himself over and over again why he couldn't produce even a simple short story. He wondered if part of his writer's block was due to fear of success. What would happen to his life if all of a sudden he became a wildly successful author? Or maybe his block was because of a fear of criticism. Writing does expose one's soul. It did seem dangerous to put one's innermost self on paper for all to see. Maybe writing wasn't such a good idea, after all.

And what about the effect writing might have on other people? The man knew authors could cause readers to take a long look at themselves in the mirror, either as individuals or as a society. Some stories might even cause readers to feel a sense of shame at what they saw in those highly polished mirrors. After all, shame can be a powerful motivator. Perhaps some writers attempt to evoke emotions in their readers, even strive to manipulate them somehow. But that kind of storytelling was not what the man had in mind. He didn't want to create stories for the sake of controlling the thoughts or actions of others.

Some of the man's friends who knew of his unwillingness to give up his passion for writing tried to show him how silly the whole thing was. But the man was certain of his desire to write and nothing his friends could do or say had any effect. He eventually came to see his friends as reflections of his own internal critic.

After a time, the man did start to receive a few rewards for his efforts. Every once in a while, the man thought to himself, *I've got it!* He would drop whatever he was doing and rush to pick up a pencil and paper or go to his typewriter. A few lines or even a paragraph or two would find their way from his mind, to his fingers, through the typewriter, and come to rest on a blank page. But it always seemed that after a brief flurry of words, the idea—with all its vividness—would evaporate. This never disappointed the man, however. In fact, he only became more determined as he started to collect more and more pieces of paper half full of his false starts.

His determination often caused him to analyze how his own mind worked. He became fascinated by the things influencing creativity. He noticed that every time he had a strong desire to write, he felt like a young boy asking his parent for permission to do something. If the imaginary parent said no to the idea, then the words stopped in their tracks and never made it on to the page. So often the thoughts offered up by his child writer became the target of his imaginary parent's scrutiny. The man soon realized this imaginary parent had stifled so many of his attempts to give birth to the stories he knew to be hiding inside his mind, afraid to come out.

He also contemplated the role his job played in this whole process. The man was employed as an editor by a small equipment manufacturer. He would take highly technical notes provided to him by the engineers responsible for inventing some new apparatus, figures and photographs given to him by a graphic artist, and ideas on style and presentation suggested to him by the Marketing Department and weave all of these things into colorful and informative brochures detailing the proper use of the equipment.

When he stepped away from the complexity and the pressures of his position, he eventually came to see himself as a creative person. He thought about the three individuals with whom he interacted the most—the engineer, the artist, and the marketer. They, too, were all very creative. But their creativity was of a different sort. He felt as though they created material out of thin air, whereas his contribution was assembly more so than synthesis. But the manner in which he assembled words, graphics, and style was a skill he had developed, nonetheless. Perhaps he could develop writing stories as a skill, as well.

As he thought about what he did at work every day, he realized the difference between the skills he utilized to produce technical brochures and his attempts to write stories was when at work there were people feeding him raw material. He would have to learn to supply his own raw material.

He wondered what the engineer, the artist, and the marketer had that he did not. He envied their energy, their artistic flair, and the way they let their intuitions guide them. He would have gladly traded a little bit of his intelligence and analytical precision for some of their creativity.

After some time, the man came to the startling conclusion that the more he examined his desire to write and his inability to concoct the novel of his dreams, the more he ended up examining his life. And the more he worked on bringing out his writing skills, the more he worked on who he was. The more the man nurtured his unfolding talents, the more he cared for himself and those parts of himself he had previously neglected. He felt very good about all of this.

Much to his surprise, the man even began praying to GOD for the creativity necessary to launch his writing career. He thought that if GOD could create an entire Universe, He must know something about creativity. He must have an unlimited supply of ideas, energy, and means to channel these gifts to those willing to be receptive. The incredible number of authors, both living and deceased, seemed to support this conclusion. The more he thought about the enormous volume of works brought into the world every day, the more he became convinced everyone must have equal access to GOD's gifts of creativity.

"GOD—if you can help me write, I would be eternally grateful," prayed the man. "Teach me, GOD, the simple art of listening to you. Please, may your creativity flow through me."

As the months tumbled by without the man finding the inspiration for which he so earnestly prayed, he met a wonderful woman and fell in love with her. She was as intelligent as she was beautiful—perfect in every way. She even understood the man's desire to write and encouraged him in his quest.

Maybe this was GOD's answer to his prayers, he thought. Here was someone who understood all he wanted, who supported all of his efforts, and who loved him unconditionally. What more could a man ask?

"Certainly, now I will find something about which to write!" exclaimed the man to his soon-to-be wife. "Love seems to fuel the imagination of so many artists and authors. With kind words from my true love, my internal critic will pack up and leave." They were soon married and lived quite happily together.

But the man's dream of writing went unfulfilled. Years went by and the man's life became full of other activities. He found himself struggling again to find the time to devote to his writing, such as it was. He rarely recited his affirmations. He again found himself asking why he wanted to write so much. And just like all the times before when he had asked this question, no answer came to him.

"Do I want to write to be famous?" he wondered one day. Fame would be a convenient shortcut to self-approval. "Or is it that I want to write to tell some great story for the purpose of entertainment? Perhaps it is to make lots of money. Or it might be that I want to use writing as a means to teach readers some valuable lesson." None of these reasons seemed to satisfy the man, and he went on about his daily business without coming to any conclusion.

He mentioned this to his wife. She listened with great attention—as she always did—but she could not offer an explanation.

Then one day, his wife made an observation. "Maybe you need to find the joy in the creative process itself. Maybe the end result of creating something isn't as important as you think. Maybe it's the adventure needing to be savored, not the destination."

Once he accepted the wisdom offered by his wife, the man discovered—quite to his surprise—he now experienced delight in a well-constructed paragraph. This simple peace coming out of nowhere slowly replaced the longing to write. He felt rather silly something so basic did what years of his fruitless efforts had not.

The man's life fell into a routine that did not involve grand dreams about writing, or more accurately, the desire to write. The man and his wife filled their lives with work and travel, family and friends, and time to devote to each other and their other interests. Pleasant though the routine was, the man sometimes wondered whether he had lost his battle with his internal critic. No—he had nothing to regret. He had not been lazy and had not procrastinated. Goodness knows he had been diligent at his desired occupation through the years, almost to the point of being obsessive. He knew his original thought of having to produce something great the first time he sat down had caused him a good deal of angst. But he had realized the power of taking baby steps and he had done that successfully. He had learned to nurture himself. He had found a loving and devoted wife.

No, there was plenty to feel good about—he had not lost any battle. Perhaps he hadn't published any stories, but he saw all of the benefits that had come from his long struggle with wanting to write. He knew for the first time that he was truly happy. He laughed at himself.

"All of these years I thought that if I became a writer I would be happy. What if—just what if—I somehow feared the writing because I feared happiness?" He grinned silently.

Then the man had an idea for a story. It wasn't like the ideas he had before. This one was towering; it burned with an intensity he had not felt before, and it caught him quite by surprise. He suddenly felt much like the child who, after persistent pleading, is allowed by the parent to engage in some long sought-after activity. The years of struggling seemed to slip away. He knew immediately what he had to do. He got up and ran into his studio, sat down, and began to write—

"There once was a man who wanted to write . . ."

——— o0o ———

"According to thy faith, be it unto you."
MATTHEW 9:29

THE LEDGE

(The Skeptic)

· · · · · · · · · · ·

THE ECHOES FROM BOOT heels striking the well-polished floors preceded the now familiar voice.

"Lights out!"

Zarce Sun De'oggo lay on his metal bunk, hands clasped firmly behind his head, anticipating the passing of the Sentinel by his cell—an obscure cell, likely one of the hundreds, even thousands, deep within the Ministry of Thought.

The guard abruptly stopped in front of the cell and glared through the shadows at its only occupant. "Offender De'oggo!" A rush of fear shot through Zarce's body.

"You best get some rest. You're scheduled to meet a Mothersoul tomorrow. She will decide your fate." With that, the figure spun on his heel and continued his metered cadence down the corridor.

"Lights out!" continued the Sentinel.

Light slowly seeped out of the aseptic hallways. Zarce hated the darkness that followed the fading footsteps. He hated the thoughts that came with the darkness even more. How many nights had it been? Zarce had lost count. He wasn't even certain it was, in fact, night. There was no way to know—there were no windows, no clocks, no means to keep track of the hour or the day in this forsaken place.

Zarce fell into his now regular pattern of questions. Why was he here? What had he done? He had not hurt anyone. He did not owe anyone any credits—he paid his bills on time. He did not imbibe in strong drink or illegal substances. Whom had he offended?

He could feel his sense of helplessness grow. He made the obligatory attempt to quell the sick feeling in the pit of his stomach. Even if he knew why he was here, he could do nothing to change his incarceration. He was utterly powerless. Of this, he was certain.

But tonight a new thought found its way into his head. He might even be grateful for the deviation from his nightly ritual, but the thought could not overpower the sense of dread this latest matter brought. What of the Mothersoul of whom the Sentinel spoke and his meeting tomorrow? Zarce thought Mothersouls served only in the Great Temples or as Head Mistresses of the Mindschools—like the one he had attended in his earlier years. He had never heard of such a Revered One sitting in judgment at some meeting. He didn't even know the purpose of this meeting—except it would, according to the Sentinel, decide his fate. In all of his time at the Ministry of Thought, no one had spoken with him or explained to him the reason for his presence or what would happen to him.

Zarce tried to think back to his days at the Mind-school, tried to recall any fragment of his memories of the

Mothersouls. He remembered catching a glimpse of one once as she hurried across a courtyard, her black robes flying as she headed into the stiff morning breeze—probably late for some assembly or convocation—her thin pale face surrounded by a narrow white cowl, her hands nowhere to be seen, no doubt buried deep within the confines of her cloak.

Even with such a rare sighting of a Mothersoul, no one spoke of such things. Not out of fear, but rather out of reverence for the Oversoul. Zarce knew precious little about Mothersouls—except, of course, what he learned at the Mindschool. He could still recall what his teachers recited from the Great Book.

"Mothersouls are the keepers of the Oversoul. They see to its every need. They are charged with keeping the purity of the flock, their minds clean, and their hearts true."

How they accomplished their awesome responsibilities, no one knew or questioned. It was part of the Great Mystery of the Oversoul. People only prayed for a roof over their heads, a good meal at the end of a day's work, and a peaceful world in which to raise their children. This was the way things had always been and would likely always be—the Oversoul permitting.

So why am I here? thought Zarce, coming back full circle. Had he done something to threaten the Order of Things, the Great Peace? How could he, one lowly worker, one loyal follower, be of any interest to the Mothersouls?

Surely the Omnipotent Oversoul and its dutiful servants, the Mothersouls, must know he had committed no offense. Zarce tried to draw some small degree of confidence from this thought as he slowly drifted off into a restless sleep.

—— o0o ——

Zarce assumed it must be morning. The Sentinel arrived at his cell with a tray containing several small cubes of bread, a bowl of cold porridge, and a metal mug of water.

"You have ten minutes to eat. Then I will be back for you," said the Sentinel.

Zarce gave thanks for the meager food and drink. He made certain none of it went to waste, so he consumed every morsel of food and drained the last sip of stale water just as the Sentinel returned.

"Say your good-byes to your cell," chided the guard. "You shan't be seeing it again."

The thought didn't bother Zarce. This cell was the tenth or twelfth one he had spent time in since his arrival. He had no possessions with him, so there was nothing to leave, nothing to carry with him.

He quickly left the cell so as not to give the Sentinel any excuse to push or shove him. During his stay, he discovered obedience to be the best approach when dealing with the guards. They only needed the slightest excuse to abuse an Offender. Zarce did not want to serve as someone's entertainment.

The Sentinel led him down a long corridor, down several flights of stairs, and finally through a series of scanners and metal detectors. They traversed two more hallways until the Sentinel directed him to enter the Inquisition Chamber. The Sentinel pointed to an old wooden chair in the first row behind a table piled high with old books and important-looking papers. As Zarce walked toward the seat indicated by the guard, he noticed two other individuals who appeared to be waiting for hearings of their own. They both sat at the back of the room. Zarce guessed his meeting with the Mothersoul would be first on the day's docket.

As soon as Zarce sat down, three stoic Clerics entered the room from a side door and stood in front of Zarce with their backs toward him, ignoring him. All wore drab green uniforms, but none of them wore the uniform particularly well. The tallest Cleric's trousers exposed hairy legs. Another stood burly and menacing with his uniform stretched tightly around his midsection. Two large wet circles radiated out from the armpits of the third Cleric, staining his shirt, signaling an obvious problem with perspiration.

"All rise," barked one of the uniformed Clerics. "The Reverend Mothersoul Minter will preside over this session and determine the fate of all Offenders."

The Mothersoul hurried into the Inquisition Chamber from a door on the opposite side. Red robes covered every part of the revered figure's body except her eyes, nose, and mouth. The robes hung loosely, not revealing any clues about the physique of this holder of obvious power. But Zarce noted her dense black eyes and the deep shadows surrounding them. Angular cheeks and mouth seemed chiseled out of cold stone. Everything in her face declared her obsession with the matters at hand with no notion of compassion or softness whatsoever.

She took several minutes to settle herself at the long wooden table situated at the front of the dimly lit room, organize her papers, and adjust the think-machine screen. Finally, she turned her head and gave a subtle nod to the overweight Cleric.

"State your case, Examiner Saathoff."

"Yes, Your Reverence," began the Cleric without pausing.

The Cleric turned around and scowled at Zarce. "Offender."

A shot of adrenaline fell to the end of his fingers. Zarce steadied himself. He didn't know the proper etiquette for this situation—he had never addressed, let alone met, a Cleric or a Mothersoul—so he said nothing. The other Clerics and Offenders took their seats.

The Cleric faced forward once again. "The Offender is charged with harboring the emotion commonly known as fear. He has willingly and knowingly allowed this emotion to dominate every facet of his life. Furthermore, because he has made decisions in response to this fear and because these decisions have adversely affected others around him, his fear has contaminated the Oversoul."

So that's it! Zarce began to understand.

The Mothersoul directed her disinterested gaze from the Examiner to Zarce. "What say you, Zarce Sun De'oggo?"

Indeed! What would he say? What should he say?

All of those days and nights in his cells—if he only knew! He could have mulled over the charges, contemplated their origin, and weighed various strategies—evaluated the pros and the cons of admitting his experience with fear. But there was no time now. There was no one with whom he could consult. He must reply to this accusation.

His mind raced. Should he admit to having felt fear? Should he deny it? How could the Examiner know what thoughts resided in the private recesses of his mind or what feelings hid in the deep places of his heart? How could a Mothersoul probe beneath his outward actions and know the extent to which his life and actions touched other people—for good or for ill? And how could an unseen Oversoul communicate whatever it knew or suspected to corporeal beings—if the Oversoul even existed? The skepticism surprised Zarce.

Fear could not be a crime, reasoned Zarce. Fear is a distraction, to be sure. Yes, but it was more than that—it was an intrusion, a liability, and a handicap. He had tried and tried repeatedly to rid himself of its unwelcome presence since he first sensed it in his heart and mind over a year ago. He didn't know how to stop it or eliminate it. He recalled his decision to minimize the possibility of contaminating others with his fear by living alone—shunning friendships and companionship. But that, of course, did nothing to address the source of the fear.

Why couldn't the fear be silent?

Zarce realized he had never fully explored the bounds of this fear, its ramifications, and what sort of trouble it might cause. But how could he have? How can one examine something one does not understand? And people do not speak of such things—there is no place safe to unwrap this emotional intruder.

But he was Of The Light! People Of The Light did not experience fear!

And now that the taste of fear was familiar to Zarce—now that he knew something of its power over one's thoughts—he could not imagine fear not being a part of everyone's daily life on this miserable little planet. Certainly, others must live in fear of something or someone, Zarce thought—especially those not Of The Light. And there must be people who create fear in those they wish to control. How can there be control without fear? And how can there be fear without anger? Is not anger an offense just as serious as fear? Zarce could not believe all of society to be simply a collection of docile individuals, existing without negative emotions. Assuming that others truly did experience fear, how did others prevent the Mothersouls from examining their minds and their thoughts? Or did they? What offenses against the Oversoul had they committed?

But fairness was not the issue at this moment. Zarce adjusted his stance and gathered his courage. He looked directly at the Mothersoul and prayed she would find the explanation of his actions—or more appropriately, his thoughts and emotions—acceptable.

"Your Reverence," he began. "I admit to having felt fear in my heart and my mind for much of the last Cycle. I did not ask for it and I tried everything I could think of to rid myself of it. I find its presence"—he paused while searching for a word—"distasteful."

The Mothersoul appeared unsympathetic. "And how did this fear find its way into your being?"

"It came because I inadvertently learned about something known as The Ledge."

Zarce noted a visible change in both the Mothersoul and the Examiner. Their spines straightened as they exchanged knowing glances with one another.

So it was right to fear this Ledge!

"What do you know of The Ledge?" exploded the Mothersoul.

A Mothersoul expressing anger? Isn't anger just as bad as fear?

"Only what I saw and what I heard one year ago," Zarce replied cautiously. "I was about to leave my apartment one evening when the young man who lived across the hall was being arrested by a pair of Sentinels. My door was open a crack, and as the confrontation started, I froze. One of the Sentinels said to my neighbor, 'We'll see how tough you are when you face The Ledge.' They led my neighbor away and I did not see him again in our building.

I didn't know what The Ledge was—I had never heard of it before. Over the next few weeks and months, I kept asking myself, what was this Ledge? Then, I began seeing this man in the market near my apartment building from time to time. Initially, I resisted the urge to ask what had happened to him—where he had gone and what he knew about The Ledge. Then one day, I could resist no more.

"I waited for him to leave the market and then approached him. I said, 'Excuse, me. Do you remember me? I used to live across the hall from you some number of months ago.' He just stared at me blankly. His face contorted and he uttered only a few words—'narrow . . . so high . . . no bottom . . . falling . . . falling.' Then he turned and ran into the crowd. I have not seen him since."

"Silence!" the Mothersoul commanded. "Enough of this talk! Further reference to The Ledge will only serve to make matters worse for you."

Zarce noticed the outburst exhausted the Mother-soul—she appeared to be catching her breath. Maybe the expression of anger weakened her somehow. Her breathing finally slowed and she steadied herself, using the table for support.

She turned her now drained gaze away from Zarce, away from the Examiner, and focused on the think-machine's screen. After a moment, a bony finger appeared from somewhere inside the robes and touched the screen.

The Mothersoul waited for several minutes. What little of her face Zarce could see suddenly filled with relief. Her head nodded ever so slightly, as if in agreement with whatever she read on the screen.

"This Tribunal has no choice but to find the Offender guilty of the charges. To answer for these charges, the

Offender will be transported to The Ledge, where he is to remain until his soul has been cleansed. The punishment is to be carried out immediately."

The words of the Mothersoul struck Zarce with astonishing force. An immediate sense of desperation and disbelief shot through him. He tried to control it—push it down—but it was no use. Blackness welled up from deep down inside him. Perhaps if he retracted his words, changed his confession. Surely there must be some way to overturn this terrible fate—something—anything.

A Sentinel nudged Zarce toward the door. He gave a meaningless glance over his shoulder as he left the Inquisition Chamber.

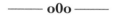

Another Sentinel led Zarce out into the hallway and down several long corridors. He quickly lost track of his location relative to the Inquisition Chamber. His head spun with the weight of his sentence.

The Offender will be transported to The Ledge—

He battled to keep walking, forcing himself to place one foot in front of the other. The pit of his stomach sickened beyond anything he had ever experienced in his life.

—where he is to remain until his soul has been cleansed!

Finally, the Sentinel stopped, turned to his right, and opened a steel door leading into a small room. The room contained a single chair in its center. An unfamiliar device hung down from the ceiling directly above the chair. A technician stood at the far side of the room and seemed to be making adjustments to an instrument-laden panel mounted on the wall. The Sentinel motioned for Zarce to enter the room, then promptly pulled the door closed behind them and locked it.

Once the technician seemed satisfied with the various settings, he glanced at the Sentinel as if to indicate the equipment was set.

The punishment is to be carried out immediately!

"Are you ready for the Offender?" asked the Sentinel.

"Affirmative." The technician nodded. "Bring him over to the chair."

Zarce wondered whether he should put up a fight, resist the Sentinel. But there were two of them, a locked door, and a maze of hallways outside with no clue as to how to exit the Ministry of Thought. Even if he could successfully navigate his way through the immense building, where would he go once he escaped? He certainly couldn't go home—or anywhere else that might be familiar to him. Did he really want to be a fugitive? No, best to get this over with—whatever *it* was.

Then he thought, *What does this chair have to do with The Ledge, anyway?* Zarce believed The Ledge to be somewhere outside—in the open air—not in some seemingly insignificant little room deep in the bowels of a huge building.

Zarce lowered himself into the chair. The technician adjusted harnesses to hold Zarce's arms in place, then reached for the inverted dome-like device overhead, tugged at it gently, guiding it down until it covered the top half of Zarce's head.

Whatever fear Zarce had experienced in the last year paled in comparison to what he felt now. He tried to prepare himself to meet his immediate future as best he could. His entire frame trembled. Sweat drenched his body. Out of the corner of his eyes, he noted the Sentinel backing away. He heard the technician flick several switches.

Suddenly, an inner sensation of tingling spread throughout his body, like electricity vibrating every fiber of his being. His awareness spiraled inward. His mind darted from thought to desperate thought. As he felt his consciousness slip away, he became increasing upset his final thoughts would be so frenzied, so scattered, so helpless—not the peaceful end he always imaged, lying in some comfortable bed, surrounded by individuals important to him.

"No!" A final, fatal mindscream faded within.

Slowly, Zarce regained consciousness. His first thought—one of gratitude that he was still alive. The machine, whatever it was, whatever it did, had not killed him. He then became aware of intense cold and the sound of howling wind. He tried to swallow, but the dryness in his throat made that impossible. He fought to open his eyes, to learn something of his surroundings.

He found he lay in the middle of a small bowl-like depression, approximately three meters in diameter. His hands sensed a cold stone floor. In the dim light, his eyes followed the contour of the rock walls as they arched up over his head to form an uneven ceiling. As he turned his head, he discovered the fourth side of the hollow open to the sky, allowing the bitter cold wind to enter.

He lay perfectly still for several minutes, desperately trying to regain his senses and his strength. The machine had robbed him of both. He began to shiver. He needed to get up and move about, perhaps find something with which he could make a fire. Forcing himself up on one elbow, he stared out the opening of his new cell.

Something was amiss, Zarce thought. Even the dim light should reveal some kind of landscape out beyond the confines of this cavern. But there was nothing. He pulled himself slowly to the opening, to the edge of the floor. Then he understood the place in which he awoke to be gouged into the side of an immense rock wall, and his little nest was high above anything else in his field of vision.

He recoiled immediately, fearing he might fall.

So this is The Ledge! There really is such a thing!

Intense horror flushed through him as he grappled to accept the desolation. Deathly afraid to move, he remained motionless for several long minutes. Zarce knew the longer he allowed fear to control his actions, the quicker he would freeze to death, but no thoughts of how to warm himself came.

He gathered his courage and again dragged himself to the opening of the cave. He turned his head from side to side. The Ledge trailed off in both directions, ending abruptly within twenty or thirty meters. When he looked out at the far horizon, Zarce did not see anything—no trace of distant mountains, no fields, no sea. Then he looked up and did not see anything in the ubiquitous ceiling of clouds above. And when he looked down, he did not detect any features in the gray mist below.

He shouted out. He waited for several long moments. No echo—no answer. He shouted again. Nothing.

An hour or two went by, and just like in his many cells at the Ministry of Thought, there was no way to gauge the passage of time. The light outside never changed. There was no day or night—no sun or moon or stars he could see. Just continual, unchanging grayness.

New sets of questions tore through his mind. What should he do? What could he do? He did not have any food or water. There did not appear to be any way down off this rock wall. He did not have any rope or anything with which to make a parachute. The face of the wall was sheer—no obvious footholds or handholds, nothing to hold on to.

Every time he raced through the same cascade of questions about his situation, he came to the same conclusion. There were only two choices: do nothing and die a slow death from the exposure and starvation and dehydration—or jump and die a quick death. He shuddered with the thought of actually allowing himself to fall. Because he could not see anything below but mist, he didn't know how long the fall would be. He might not be able to see the bottom until he reached it. But then again, what if no bottom existed? What if he kept falling and falling? He would still die of exposure and starvation and dehydration.

There must be a bottom! How could there not be?

The growing numbness in his hands and feet forced him to consider a second set of questions that demanded his attention. If he decided to jump, when would he do it? How much of the cold could he endure while gathering his courage? How much longer could he tolerate the cries from his empty stomach and parched mouth? Indeed— when should he jump? Now? An hour from now? What preparations did he need to make? What could he possibly think about he had not already thought about dozens of times before? There was only one thing to focus on—the very act of jumping. Only in his wildest imaginings of what The Ledge might be had he conjured up this scenario. In the luxury of his thoughts, he recalled his solution was simply to pull his mind away from such a dilemma—to ignore the need to find an answer to the situation. But now, here he was—facing it. How does one prepare for such a thing?

Zarce laid his head back down on the cold stone, closed his eyes, and cried. It was then he remembered seeing his former neighbor in the marketplace. He had survived this place. Yes, there must be a way out. But did he jump or did he stay on The Ledge? Zarce recalled his neighbor's words—"narrow . . . so high . . . no bottom . . . falling . . . falling." He must have jumped. But how did he survive? How did he find his way back after being here? Something did not seem right. None of this made any sense. Zarce saw only death at each option.

Why prolong thought for the sake of being able to think for a few more minutes?

Zarce searched desperately for the strength to make the ultimate decision. More importantly, he searched for the fortitude to allow himself to fall off of The Ledge.

"Damn you!" Zarce screamed out. "Is this how the great-and-powerful Oversoul treats its worshippers? Its subjects? Do you so doubt your power to control us that you must torture us, treat us as if we're a fragile puppet—your plaything to do with whatever it is you wish? And how is this supposed to cleanse my soul, pray tell?"

Zarce paused to catch his breath. Not sure if it was because of the altitude or his fear, but he was ghastly tired. He realized he hadn't slept since before his hearing in front of the Mothersoul. Soon, he thought, there would no longer be a need for sleep.

"I will claim my power over you," he continued. "I will deny you your pleasure. I will rid myself of you and my fear once and for all."

Zarce closed his eyes, leaned forward, and rolled over the edge.

Immediately, he felt the rushing air against his face and hands. The air was bitter cold. He fell faster and faster. He opened his eyes one last time and looked up, but saw no trace of the dreaded Ledge. He managed to rotate himself in the intense wind rushing up to sap what little warmth remained in him. He tried to peer down into the mist. He saw nothing—just more mist.

In his last instant, he finally realized the true nature of The Ledge—what it had been for the last year. It was fear. It was that simple. He now understood what one must do to control one's fear—what one must do to eliminate it. He also understood he had made the right decision.

Then it ended.

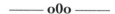

Zarce awoke in his bedroom. And just as he did every morning, he reached over to his video station and pressed the button to begin the morning's news visi-cast.

"And today is the twenty-sixth day of Avrinne, the thirty-seventh cycle of the reign of Queen Addix. Here are today's top stories."

The twenty-sixth day of Avrinne, thought Zarce. He felt as though something was out of sync, maybe even that memories of the previous day—or days—were clouded somehow. He tried to think about the last week—the last month—and remember what he did, but all that came to mind were dreams of falling. *My mistake—it was just a dream*, he thought. *Everything is fine.*

—— o0o ——

"Say to those who are of a fearful heart,
'Be strong, do not fear! Here is your GOD. He will come with
vengeance, with terrible reward. He will come and save you.'"

ISAIAH 35:4

MICROWAVE MAN

(The Survivor)

* * * * * * * * * * * *

IS THE SIGN STILL THERE? *That is the question.*

Years ago I made scores of trips through the heartland of Virginia. I had grown up in Maryland and had opted to attend a small college in North Carolina. Rather than fight the maddening traffic and hours of featureless driving on the interstates, I chose to add on an extra hour to the trip and head straight through the Piedmont region of the state. I enjoyed immersing myself in the beauty offered by a two-lane road that rarely had much traffic on it and provided some truly awe-inspiring vistas of rolling hills and pine-filled woods. After these excursions up and down my route of choice, I came to know the names of all of the towns and had adopted various landmarks as a way to help pass the time during the six-hour drive.

One such little town was Ordonsville—quite typical of the dozen or so rural towns along my favorite one-hundred-mile stretch of road. Old southern-style homes lined the sides of the highway as one neared the main intersection. The homes were interrupted by an occasional church. Closer to the center of town was the post office, a grocery store, a library, and a Civil War museum. Just before the solitary traffic light was a row of antique shops—all renovated to help attract the curious traveler wanting to take a break from driving and browse through what were, no doubt, contents from the homes of residents now citing the local cemetery as their current address.

As I would leave these familiar places behind on my way south, there was always one metal sign piquing my curiosity. Perched on a narrow strip of grass between the road and a plain white two-story house, the sign simply read "Microwave Man" in neatly printed black letters.

Now—mind you—I have always been a fan of superhero comic books and movies, so my imagination would go to work at this point, trying to determine just exactly what this mystery man might look like, what primary colors his costume might be, and whether he had any superpowers. As I passed by the sign, I would say to myself, *someday, I am going to stop, go in, and see what this fellow is all about.*

I never did.

That was then. Many years have passed since those trips through Ordonsville. And—oh yes—I did manage to graduate from college and have been fortunate enough to eke out a living as a writer. Several months ago, though, I wrapped up my final big assignment for my employer and submitted my letter of resignation. I decided it was time to slow things down and focus on my two passions—traveling and writing short stories. My first thought, quite unexpectedly, was about my favorite drive—to North Carolina, through Ordonsville, and past that sign. I made arrangements to be gone for a few weeks and secured a reservation at one of the inns at the edge of town. What happened during my stay there is what this story is all about. Believe it if you wish—but even if you don't, there is some truth in it.

Thirty miles after leaving the interstate, I started seeing the old familiar landmarks dotting the landscape outside of Ordonsville. The Pizza Hut five miles north of town was now boarded up. Some of the old homes wore dark mold and coats of unkempt ivy. A retirement home now sat just on the outskirts of the corporate limits. My favorite restaurant and sandwich shop were gone. The sign in front of the Ordonsville Methodist Church announced a long past event. The more things I saw, the more I feared Ordonsville had succumbed to the same decline so many other towns had over the last fifty years. Most of all, I feared the Microwave Man and his sign would no longer be there.

When planning my trip, I found there were three inns in Ordonsville from which to choose. I picked the one closest to the south side of town—closest to the Microwave Man's location. I quickly found the establishment and turned into the driveway lined with a split rail fence on my left and beds of carefully landscaped flowers and bushes on my right. After checking in and hauling my few bags up to my room, I put on my hiking boots, slung my camera over my left shoulder, and retrieved my backpack and walking stick from the back of my van. I set off at a brisk pace, heading down a neighborhood street back out to the main road, just a block from my destination. As I marched along,

I started thinking about how silly this journey of mine might seem to my friends. Funny thing about wishing for time to do all of the little things you can't squeeze in during your busy working life—when you finally have the time, the little things seem almost trivial.

I connected with the main road, turned to my left, and there it was—the sign.

Praise Jesus!

As I found my way up the broken sidewalk to the front of the Microwave Man's address, I realized the majority of my thinking over the last hours, days, and weeks had been focused on simply whether the sign would still be claiming its territory alongside the road. I really hadn't spent much time planning what I would do should the sign actually still be present.

I made the one step up onto the porch and another three steps to the front door. I looked around the perimeter of the door for a doorbell button but didn't find one. I bent backward for a moment to look in the windows to see if there might be a light on in the front room or if the drapes were open or closed. No lamp was on, but the drapes were open. I came to the conclusion that if this was indeed a business establishment, the proprietor would certainly expect folks to walk in—and that is exactly what I did.

There was something a bit odd about the front room. While it seemed dim, the pale green walls were almost iridescent—a subtle glow hung on them. An old sofa—with antique lamps perched atop end tables at each end—filled the wall to my right. A simple desk and chair were situated on the wall to my left. A customer service counter ran the width of the room along the far wall. A solitary door—just slightly ajar—was behind the left end of the counter. A large picture surrounded by a simple wooden frame hung in the center of the back wall. I wasn't certain if the image was a painting or a print, but whatever it was, it was captivating.

A shoreline extended from the left foreground to the right background, receding on a diagonal path. The surf looked calm—a shallow wash of pale white foam was present. Overhead was a stretch of an early twilight sky with what appeared to be a smattering of stars, densely packed in places—perhaps a section of the Milky Way—and evidence of a recent sunset present on the right side. But the thing holding my gaze was the water. The section of ocean filling the left side seemed a golden green, if that made any sense. And it, too, emanated a strange shimmer, giving one the sense the water was gently moving back and forth, ever so slowly.

I stood transfixed, staring at this strange panorama. At that moment, the proprietor emerged from the back room and stepped up to the counter, placing his small hands on the polished wood.

"May I assist you?" came the timid voice.

I turned away from the painting—or the print or whatever it was—and looked at the man. He was short—no taller than five feet—bald and had simple features. I couldn't guess his age, but I knew the sign out front had been there for at least forty years. His clothes were all the same color—almost the same hue as the water in the painting—and they, too, seemed to have a subtle glow about them.

He then turned his head around to his left and looked up at the picture.

"Captivating, isn't it?" he said.

"Um—yes," I managed. "Are you the Microwave Man?" As I heard myself ask the question, I thought how socially awkward it sounded. "I'm sorry—let me tell you why it is I ask." I leaned my walking stick against the counter and removed my glasses.

"Many years ago I would drive by your place on my way to and from college. I always said I would stop in and see what was here. Your sign—it was . . . curious. I could never quite figure out what it meant, or what it was you sold, or what service it was you offered. I'm now retired with ample time to travel. I remembered my pledge and so I drove down for a stay in Ordonsville and, well, here I am."

I made a mental note that I didn't see anything in the room even vaguely related to microwaves or even anything electronic—no ovens or communication devices.

The man simply smiled at me. Then he began to nod his head gently up and down; it seemed to be mimicking the imaginary ebb and flow of the tide in the picture.

"Yes—and don't feel bad for asking me. You are not the first person to do so."

"Okay, thanks for that." I waited for something else from him, but he offered nothing. "So, just exactly what is it you do here—or sell here?" And then I added, "If you don't mind me asking."

"Not at all. I don't actually sell anything and I don't really provide any service—at least not in a traditional sense. I simply collect things—anything that emits microwaves. That's it."

Really—that's it? After all these years?

"So, for example, if I had a broken microwave oven, I could bring it to you, and you would take it off my hands?"

"That's right," he replied.

"Is any money exchanged one way or the other?" I queried.

"No."

"And so what is it exactly that you do with old microwave ovens and such?" *This is starting to get interesting*, I thought.

"Ah, yes—that is the question, isn't it?" The man flashed his polite smile at me once again. "That would take a bit of explaining. Meet me here again one week from today."

With that, the little man turned and made his way to the door leading to the back room.

I wasn't quite sure what to do or what to say at this point. So I retrieved my walking stick, put my glasses back on, and found my way to the front door, pulling it closed behind me as I reentered the bright Virginia afternoon.

I walked around town, getting the lay of the land as my dad used to say whenever he went someplace new. I found the grocery store, the courthouse, and the local bar. After an hour or two, I returned to the B&B to clean up, got back in my van, and headed due west to a microbrewery I had read about in a recent AAA magazine. It was the first day they were serving food and, despite unnecessary apologies from my waiter, everything was quite good. And even though the pilsner was most tasty, I resisted the urge to have a second.

When I returned to the B&B, I found the proprietor in the cozy living room finishing up some paperwork at her desk. She was a middle-aged woman—or maybe a few years past middle aged as her hair was starting to make the transition from dirty blond to gray and the skin on her face had started to collect wrinkles.

"Excuse me, ma'am," I said. "Do you have a few minutes to answer some questions for me?" I didn't mean to interrupt her, but curiosity about this afternoon's meeting with the Microwave Man was in overdrive.

"Of course," she answered. "My apologies for not being here when you checked in earlier today. I do hope my daughter saw to your needs."

"Oh, yes—she did. Everything is fine and the room is most comfortable." I sat down in the chair next to her desk and continued. "I had a nice walk this afternoon. I was trying to familiarize myself with Ordonsville as I've never actually stayed here before, though I've driven through it more times in my life than I can count."

Her blue eyes seemed fixated on me, waiting for my next words.

"Do you mind if I ask you how long you've lived in Ordonsville? I am a writer and I'm doing some background research for a book I am working on."

Okay, so I am lying about this last statement.

"Oh, not at all. Glad to help." She put her pen down and shifted a bit in her desk chair. "My late husband and I moved to Ordonsville about twenty years ago. It was sort of a lifelong dream to head south and run a bed and breakfast. Jim—that was his name, my husband's name—he passed away twelve years ago. That's when my daughter's marriage fell apart and she moved down here to live with me. I'm so grateful to have her company. Not every parent gets along with their grown children and vice versa, you know."

"I'm sorry to learn of your husband's passing. That must have been tough," I offered.

"Oh, it was," she said. "But you know, life moves on and time does heal."

"As I was out strolling about this afternoon, I came across an interesting sign. I was wondering if you knew anything about it. Out on the highway—about six blocks south of the center of town—there is a white metal sign with black letters. It simply says, 'Microwave Man.' Do you know anything about the business or its owner?"

I crossed my fingers, hoping she might enlighten me.

She stared at the ceiling for a moment. "You know, funny thing about that—the sign, I mean, not your question—the sign has been there ever since I've lived here and I am not at all certain I've ever run across the person who lives there. I've heard some say it is a man, that he rarely ventures out, and that he is—how shall we say—a bit eccentric?"

"Any idea what sort of business this gentleman runs?" I paused for a second. "I can't quite figure out whether he sells things related to microwaves—presumably ovens—or whether he provides some sort of service, perhaps fixing microwave ovens. But I would think these days it would be cheaper to simply just go out and buy a new oven rather than trying to get one's broken oven fixed."

"I see your point. Perhaps you might find out something at the local newspaper—the *Ordonsville Gazette*—over on East Main Street. Or you might try the Chamber of Commerce a few doors down from there."

"I'll do that. Thank you—both very good ideas. Good night, ma'am." With that, I headed upstairs to my room for some much-needed sleep.

—— o0o ——

The next morning I awoke with a mind full of questions about this Microwave Man. What was his story? What did he do? How could I find out more about him? The suggestions the innkeeper made on the previous evening came to the forefront of my thoughts.

I got out of bed, got dressed, and headed downstairs for breakfast. The innkeeper's daughter served me coffee, orange juice, and a bowl of steaming hot oatmeal with fresh strawberries cut up and neatly arranged. A choice of local honey and brown sugar was on the table. I was left in the dining room to contemplate my plans for the day in silence. Apparently, I was the only guest at the inn.

After breakfast, I headed back upstairs to brush my teeth and retrieve my backpack, camera, and hiking stick, then back downstairs, out the front door, and out into the crisp morning air.

I decided to start my day at the offices of the local newspaper. It wasn't hard to find. Ordonsville is not a terribly big place and its residents are all quite knowledgeable about where everything is and most willing to help an obvious stranger to these parts.

A small bell chimed as I opened the door to the newspaper's office. A customer service counter was just inside, piled high with various stacks of bundled newspapers, each with a small tag on it and the name of someone inscribed on it. One might assume the names belonged to paper boys— or paper girls, as the case may be.

A polite young lady dressed in blue jeans and a print top got up from behind her desk and made her way over to greet me. "And how may I help you today?" Her pronunciation of the word *help* gave away her strong southern accent.

"Yes," I began, not quite certain how to proceed. "I am a writer and am doing some research on a story about the Virginia Piedmont." I didn't really want to start off with direct questions about my true target. "I guess my first question is whether or not you all have an archive of your past issues and, if so, how far back do they go?"

"Well now," she said as she gestured for me to follow her down the short hallway to a room in the back of the building. "This is our library—if you want to call it that. We have copies of everything we've printed for the last thirty years. Why don't you have a seat and help yourself? I'll be up front if you need anything. Don't hesitate to ask."

She turned and left me with three decades worth of newspapers to sort through.

Where do I start?

I located the oldest issues and randomly picked out one from December 1985—several years after I graduated from college and, therefore, several years after I stopped making periodic treks through town. I quickly scanned the dozen pages, looking for any mention of "microwaves"— though I didn't really expect to find any, especially since the innkeeper didn't know much about this Microwave Man. It struck me I might have better luck if I reviewed the ads— perhaps there might be some sort of advertisement with the word *microwave* in it.

No luck with the first issue—or the second or the third. As I looked around I discovered the newspaper had compiled indexes for each six-month period with a short summary of what stories appeared and when. The indexes did save me a great deal of time, but they didn't yield any answers.

I also noticed a map of Ordonsville hanging on one of the walls. I searched for the house where I'd been the previous afternoon and got the address. This, I decided, might prove useful at my next stop—the county courthouse.

I packed up my things and headed back out the hall-way. The young lady looked up at me and asked, "Did you find anything useful?"

"Actually, I might have. And now that I know what resources you have available, I just might be back. Thanks so much for your time."

"Oh, you're welcome. Enjoy your stay here," she said, adding a few too many vowels to the word *here*. I turned and headed back out onto the street and to the courthouse next door.

Upon entering the county courthouse building, I found a directory posted up on the wall. I wanted to start my search for information in the Department of Finance, thinking they would have records on who paid property taxes and for how long. I followed the signs leading me up to the second floor.

The door to the office was open. Several women were performing the usual administrative chores—punching of holes, stapling, and filing. None of them looked up—they were probably pretty used to having folks make themselves at home in the adjacent room filled with stacks of plat books. And while looking at plat books had been my original plan, I quickly changed my thinking when I saw a computer ter-minal sitting on a table just inside the waiting area. Signs made it clear anyone could use it, and it was available.

I pulled the chair out, set my backpack on the floor, and sat down. I took out the piece of paper on which I had scribbled the Microwave Man's address and entered the house number and street into the appropriate fields. A fresh screen containing the property address, a property description—which included the name of the sub-development—and an account number popped up. I clicked on the hyperlink embedded in the account number. And there, on the next screen, appeared the name of the Microwave Man—Aura Verte. *Sort of an odd name*, I thought.

I also noted he had owned the property for as far back as the electronic records went. A short statement was included at the bottom of the page. It said if one was looking for information from earlier years, a request form would have to be filed with the County Clerk. But I had what I needed—a name and confirmation the Microwave Man had, in fact, lived in the home for at least thirty years.

Before heading back to the B&B, I decided to make one last stop—the library. It took ten minutes to walk the several blocks across town. This fellow's name perplexed me and I wanted to see if there might be a computer with access to the Internet.

With this being a small town, it wasn't totally surprising the library wouldn't open until noon—and it was eleven forty-five. So I headed across the street to the local hardware store. One of the items on my to-do list was to find out if anyone knew of a hiking trail that would take me up to Boswell's Bluff—a rocky outcropping about two miles due west of town. Around these parts, such things are called monadnocks. I thought it might offer a nice view of the surrounding countryside.

An elderly gentleman with frizzy gray hair and matching mustache sat behind an old-style cash register.

"Well, you don't see many of these things anymore," I said, pointing to the machine.

"Nope. That you surely don't. Shame, too. All of the electronic gizmos these days—I don't know if I trust the stuff."

"You got that right," I agreed, trying to be friendly.

"Now what can I do ya for?"

"I'm spending a few days in your wonderful little town and wanted to take a hike up to Boswell's Bluff this afternoon to take a gander at the view. I hear it is supposed to be pretty nice. Was wondering if you might know where the trailhead is—assumin' of course, there is a trail."

"Oh, there's a trail, ol' right. Been up that way many times—though not recently. My knees are getting too sore for the trek. But . . ." He was lost in thought for a moment. "Oh, yes—the trailhead. Follow Second Street out until it ends on the west side of town—just a few blocks from here, so ya don't need to drive or nothin'. You look like you're in pretty good shape. Should only take ya about an hour to reach the bluff."

"Thanks—much obliged."

As I turned to go out, he said, "Enjoy the hike."

"I plan on it!"

Just as I got back to the library, a rather plump woman dressed in a tight-fitting jumper was unlocking the front door.

"Good timing," she said to me while putting away her keys. "Just give me a moment to turn on the lights. Can I help you find anything?"

"I thought maybe the library might have a computer with access to the Internet. I'm a writer and trying to do a little research. My laptop doesn't seem to find any Wi-Fi around here."

"Right over there." She pointed. "Help yourself."

"Thanks."

I turned on the machine. It seemed as though Ordonsville was not quite caught up with the rest of the world in its ability to connect quickly to the information superhighway.

Several thoughts regarding the name Aura came to me as I was waiting for the Internet to come up on the computer screen. Once the search engine appeared, I typed in the letters *a-u-r-a*. There was the obvious term used to describe the "distinctive atmosphere or quality that seems to surround and be generated by a person, thing, or place." Other references reminded me that *aura* was a French word—the future tense of the verb *avoir*, meaning "will have." And I couldn't help but think it sounded like another French word—*or*, meaning "gold." Then I typed in the last name—Verte. More references to French—*verte*, meaning "green."

Green aura? Representing the color of nature and health and balance? Gold green? Will have green? Was there any significance to his name?

Thoughts of green and gold took me back to the waiting room at Aura's home and the subtle glow from the walls and from the captivating framed picture.

Okay, now this really is starting to get interesting, I thought. *But time for lunch.*

The trailhead was right where the gentleman in the hardware store said it would be. A well-trodden path zigzagged its way up a gently sloping field until it disappeared in a grove of pine trees. Once under the cover of the dense branches, the narrow pathway became filled with roots and rocks, forcing me to look down so as not to trip or stumble. I relied on my hiking stick to help me with each new step up.

As I continued to climb, I thought I heard something in the distance. It didn't take long to realize there was a stream somewhere off to my right. The sound of water falling over boulders soon drowned out the crunch of my footsteps. After another bend in the trail, I was greeted by a staircase of small pools, each one emptying into the next. My gaze followed the water up the hillside for as far as the trees would allow. I smiled at the thought of hiking alongside this wondrous sight.

The path eventually veered away to the left and led to the base of a set of stairs constructed from stones neatly pieced together. Images of dwarves from Middle Earth came to mind. My knees let out a silent groan as I estimated the length and inclination of the next bit of my ascent. But up I went until I reached what appeared to be a ridge. The trail made a sharp turn to the left, and—within a few minutes—I found myself on Boswell's Bluff, staring out at the countryside many hundreds of feet below.

It took me a couple of moments to orient myself. The sun was off to my right and slightly behind me, meaning I was looking eastward. I easily found the cluster of buildings and homes making up Ordonsville and saw the ribbon of road winding its way down from the north and retreating off to the south.

I took off my backpack, unzipped it, and reached inside for my binoculars. After adjusting the magnification and focusing the lens, I started looking at Ordonsville. Based on my walk around town earlier in the day, I identified the major landmarks. I located the B&B where I was staying and followed the street out to the main highway. One block up and there was the home of the Microwave Man—Aura's home.

Holy moly—what is that?

Because his house also faced east, I was looking at the back of his home. I refocused the binoculars just to make certain I was really seeing what I was seeing. There—in his backyard—was a reasonably large parabolic dish antenna, perhaps ten or twelve feet in diameter. There were three equally spaced supports reaching in from the rim of the disk to the feedhorn located at the focal point of the dish. Much to my surprise, this dish was not pointed skyward as one might expect if the device were being used to capture television signals from a geosynchronous satellite. Rather, it appeared to be pointed at a microwave tower sitting atop a hill just off to my left.

More questions for this Microwave Man, I thought.

A week passed. I did some writing. I did some hiking. I did some more research. But mostly I thought about Aura—the Microwave Man—and about our next encounter. The time passed slowly, but when the week was up, I made my way back out to the main road, up one block, and to the front door of Aura's home. Still feeling a bit odd about walking in, I again reminded myself this was a business—well, sort of. I went in.

Everything was as it was before, except this time, the strange man was sitting in one of the chairs along the front wall. He motioned to me to come and sit in the other chair, which I did.

"You have questions," he said very matter-of-factly. "You have spent time since we last met trying to learn more about me, yes?"

"That's true," I answered, wondering if my queries had been that obvious. "It just seemed like one question led to another and before I knew it—"

"Oh, it's okay. I'm not upset. In fact, I am amused someone would be so curious about me." A hint of a smile seemed to cross his face.

"Okay, then," I said. "Let's start at the beginning. Your name, Aura Verte—assuming that is your name—tell me more about that. Is it French?"

The Microwave Man smiled again. "It is my name. And not your run-of-the-mill name, is it? I'm afraid you would have to ask my parents why they chose it for me. But—as you may have concluded—it does mean 'gold green.'"

"And where are you from?"

"Nowhere around here. My parents were from Aurillia."

"Aurillia? I'm not familiar with it."

"Like I said, it is nowhere around here."

I didn't feel like I was making much progress.

"And how long have you lived in Ordonsville? The records at the courthouse would seem to suggest you have been here for as long as the records go back."

"You are correct. But the older records likely refer to my father. He had the same name. My parents . . . they . . . arrived here many years ago."

There was something about the way Aura uttered the phrase "arrived here" that sounded a bit out of place. I decided to ask the question I started to ask at the end of my last visit here.

"Last week I asked you what it was you did with the old microwave devices you collect."

"Ah, yes," he answered. "How shall we say—I am building something. I disassemble the old microwave ovens—and cellular phones—and use certain parts for my . . . project."

I wonder if this has anything to do with the satellite dish I saw.

"Several days ago, I took a hike—climbed up to the overlook, Boswell's Bluff. Beautiful up there—quite a view of the countryside." I thought I would see if I might get Aura to offer up something without asking the real question.

"Yes, it is. I have made the hike before." No further commentary followed his statement.

"I'm reasonably certain you can guess one of the things I saw while I was up there? That being the large satellite dish in your backyard?"

Still no response.

"I couldn't help but notice the dish was aimed at the large microwave tower sitting up on the next ridge. I'm just curious about what you do with the dish."

A minute passed with the two of us looking at one another.

"Come back again tomorrow," said Aura. "I think you will get the answers you are looking for."

Aura then stood up and walked out of the room.

—— oOo ——

Once again, I found myself not quite certain what to do, so I got up, gathered my things, and left. Back out on the street, I decided to return to the library and its access to the Internet. I looked at my watch. Three fifteen. Still time to get there before it closed at four o'clock.

Walking briskly, I completed the crosstown trek within fifteen minutes. I gave a quick wave to the librarian and headed straight back to the computer table. No one was using it—praise Jesus. The machine was already on and the search application was on the screen. I typed in the word Aurillia.

Nothing. Somehow I was not surprised.

Next, I tried searching for Aurillia on various map software applications.

Still nothing.

Just exactly where is this Aurillia, anyway?

I sat there and thought for a few minutes, but couldn't come up with any other searches. So, I picked up my backpack, gave a farewell nod to the librarian, and headed back to the B&B. I wasn't sure what to make of what I had learned from Aura and wasn't sure what my next move should be—except, of course, tomorrow's visit to the Microwave Man. Perhaps a good night's sleep might help clear my thoughts.

I went to bed a little after eleven o'clock. The soft sheets and the cool night air made it easy to fall asleep. While I was off in dreamland, something very strange happened. A flash of extremely intense light filled the room and woke me up. It was so blinding that even with my eyes closed, I found myself instinctively raising my hand to shield my eyes. And an instant later, it was gone.

I looked at the clock on my nightstand. It was blinking on and off. The time was 2:27 A.M. The fact that the display was blinking suggested the power had gone off—presumably at the same instant as the brilliant flash of light.

I laid my head back down on the pillow and wondered if the incident had actually happened—or had I just been dreaming? I'm not sure what resolution I came to because I quickly fell back asleep.

The next morning I woke up to find the clock still blinking. So I knew that at least part of what I remembered had really happened. But the light? I wasn't sure about that.

When I went down for breakfast, I asked the innkeeper whether she had experienced anything unusual during the night. While she did confirm the power had been off for a brief moment, she didn't report anything about the bright flash of light.

By the end of breakfast, I came to the conclusion my next visit to Aura couldn't wait until the afternoon. My gut told me Aura was somehow connected to the night's unusual occurrences. It was time for some answers.

I stepped down from the front porch of the B&B. A strange stillness had descended upon the town. The now familiar neighborhood street seemed devoid of chirping birds and the rustle of leaves I had heard on previous walks. *Something has happened*, I told myself.

I rounded the corner and headed up to Aura's home. This time I didn't hesitate to open the front door and walk in. No one was in the front room. I quickly noticed the curious radiance coming from the walls gone. I looked up at the picture hanging at the center of the rear wall—its mystical allure also gone. It was now just a painting of a seashore scene, one you might see in the waiting room of a doctor's office.

"Aura?" I called out.

No response.

"Aura," I said in a louder voice.

Again, no response.

I ducked under the break in the customer service counter and headed for the door leading to the back room. It was slightly ajar. As I pushed it open, I was amazed at what I saw. There were shelves from floor to ceiling all around the entire room. On every shelf was a piece of electronic equipment and wires running every which way, connecting the pieces of equipment to one another. In the center of the room was a wooden table with more equipment stacked underneath it and wires running up to a computer situated on its surface.

All of the lights in all of the panels, however, were dark, and the computer screen was blank. It was then I noticed a single sheet of paper sitting on top of the computer keyboard. In very neat handwriting was a note that read:

Dear Friend—

By now, you have figured out Aurillia is not a place on this Earth, but rather is a place far, far away. My parents came from there many years ago. My whole life I have been dreaming about how to find my way to the place they called home.

And by now, you have probably realized the antenna behind my home is not for receiving signals, but is for sending them. I have been collecting parts and pieces of equipment to use in the building of a giant radio of sorts—one that permitted me to send a signal to those who have come looking for me. As I write this note, I know that my people will be coming for me soon and will be taking me home—home to a place I have never been.

Know that regardless of where we are from, we are all points of light, shining bright white deep within.

One day, when your spirit releases its hold on your physical body, you will find your soul has the means to travel anywhere in this Universe—instantly. I hope you will pay a visit to Aurillia. You may have guessed the picture in the living room was of Aurillia—a place of gold-green seas and gentle beings.

May the Eternal Light bless your days.
Aura

I walked outside with Aura's note in my hand. I looked up at the sky, half expecting something to happen, some sign from Aura that he was up there—somewhere—looking down on me. It was then I realized the "Microwave Man" sign was gone. At least I had my answers. I now knew about the Microwave Man.

Bon voyage, Aura.

—— o0o ——

"Ye are all the children of light,
and the children of the day:
we are not of the night, nor of darkness."
1 THESSALONIANS 5:5

AN INTRICATE BALANCE

(The Saint and The Sinner)

. . . .

"HOW CAN YOU BE SO sure?" interrogated Father Trallix, disturbed this strange woman was trying to convince him of something no one could possibly know for certain.

"Trust me, Father, I know," she said firmly. "Your life is in danger. Your faith is suffocating—that is, unless we correct the situation. We have the opportunity to do that here—now. But only if you accept what I'm about to tell you." He looked more destitute than she had imagined.

"We all die, my child. You're telling me nothing I didn't already know." Trallix rubbed the stubble clinging to his unkempt chin. He studied her gracefulness and sensed a hint of urgency in the shadowy blue of her eyes. "Besides, I don't fear death. I am quite prepared to die. As for my faith, what business is it of yours, anyway?"

"I assure you, Father, I have more of a vested interest in whether you live or die than you might think. If you can spare some of your precious time, I'll gladly expound upon why." The accent told Trallix his unexpected guest had not been born into the more highly educated upper echelons of interstellar society.

Trallix laughed with pained effort. His outburst reverberated off the chill walls of the castle that had served his order for over nine hundred years. "Hey, I've got no place to go. This wonderful asylum grants me all the time I want."

"All right, then." Sister Othrosa Vella pulled up a wooden chair close to the recluse. She gathered the lower portion of her heavily starched habit and sat down. The late afternoon sun had made her sweat as she climbed the final steps to the ancient fortress. She felt the dampness against her back. She calmly folded her hands and closed her tired eyes. In the half-light of a solitary lamp, Trallix could see that she whispered a prayer. A moment later, she continued.

"You and I are related. Not genetically, mind you. Not like a brother and sister. But spiritually. I know how this must sound, but our two souls are linked together by a bond I don't fully comprehend myself."

"Soul mates!" Trallix snapped. "Right! I should be so lucky as to find a woman such as yourself!" He caught himself trying to imagine what his visitor might look like underneath the black robe. No doubt she exuded a certain enticing quality. Her cheekbones were higher than most women's, her eyes more widely spaced. Thick dark eyebrows framed the top of her face—her jaw firm, her chin slightly pointed. She spoke with a deep, silky voice. Even though he couldn't tell the color of her hair, he decided she must be a rather handsome woman.

"No," said Vella patiently. "We are not linked in a romantic sense, either. We're like yin and yang—two sides of the same coin."

"This is nonsense!"

"Let me be more precise. We are two counter-weights on opposite sides of an intricate spiritual balance, you and me. According to the First Theorem of Spiritual Mechanics, a soul can appear spontaneously out of nothing provided a corresponding soul of equal and opposite presence appears at the exact same time."

"I've heard of such a theorem. It's pure fantasy. Wishful thinking for academically idle minds. And even if true, you have no proof! And you call yourself one of the faithful! Ha!"

"Then consider this. You and I are exactly the same age. True we were born on different planets, but we were born at the exact same instant in time. I've checked the archives. I have copies of the documents if you wish to see them."

"How did you ever come up with this absurd notion, anyway? And why did you drag me into it?"

Vella patiently shook her head from side to side. "No. That's not it at all. Now, if you're quite done, I'll answer your question."

"I'm listening," said Trallix, holding his irritation in check.

"I began studying on Vatican Prime under Mother Superior Aarthra ten years ago. She introduced me to spiritual mechanics, and I became completely enthralled with the subject. I spent every spare moment I could in the university library, reading every computer file and every ancient text on it. The more I read, the more I realized how limited the body of knowledge was and how many unanswered questions remained.

"But the concept that fascinated me the most was the First Theorem of Spiritual Mechanics. Orgona Mannossa proposed it three centuries ago but was never able to test it—and how could one test it? There were a hundred billion people spread across a dozen worlds. It would be impossible to find two people who were born and who died at the exact same moments in time. And now, several hundred years later, there are over half a trillion people alive on almost fifty planets!

"While it's true the human population has continued to flourish, so has its technology. I decided that the vast resources of Vatican Prime just might give me the tools I needed to prove or disprove this theory. So I approached Mother Superior Aarthra with my plan."

"And what did the old windbag have to say? Did she think you a raving lunatic?"

"Quite the contrary. She was intensely curious. She gave me access to everything I needed. I programmed the Vatican's Unitronic Database to search for individuals who had been born at the exact same instant. What I found amazed me. There were billions of pairs of individuals. There were also an equally large number of unpaired names, but I attributed that to incomplete or corrupt information in the database.

"Then one day, quite on a whim, I decided to check my own name and asked to see a list of all those who were born at the exact same moment as me. Not surprisingly, a rather large collection of names emerged."

"Then how did you determine that out of all those souls, mine was your 'equal and opposite soul'?"

"A legitimate question. Especially since there's so much depending on me convincing you that we are a connected pair," admitted Vella. She felt maybe, just maybe, Trallix was beginning to take her assertion seriously. "First, I asked the computer to eliminate individuals who had already died. That got rid of about half of the names. But then I became stumped. It wasn't until days later when I had a major revelation.

"There is a balance in the Spiritual Universe. Sages might refer to it as order and disorder, harmony and chaos. But I prefer to think of the fabric of the Spiritual Universe in terms of a kind of semitransparent mirror, like the surface of a large body of water—except without any shoreline. Below the surface, there is an infinitely deep ocean of pure water. Above, there is an equally infinite sky, crystal clear.

"Think of our two souls in this very simple place. One soul swimming in the depths, the other floating through the sky. Both souls equally distant from the surface. And because the souls are equal and opposite, if the soul in the ocean falls to new depths, the other soul soars. The opposite is true, as well. If the one soul flies higher, the deeper the other must go."

"That's rubbish! You expect me to believe any of this is true? You're the crazy one here, not me," wheezed Trallix in a strained voice.

"No, listen," Sister Vella pleaded. "It's important you understand. It's your soul that's at stake here! You're the one sinking deeper and deeper."

"I don't see any point in this," protested the holy man. "I will die and that is that!" Trallix said, almost bragging.

"That's precisely why I'm here." Vella closed her eyes again and uttered another prayer, this one more frantic. "Please let me finish."

Trallix waved his hand in a circular motion as if to encourage Vella to finish her aimless treatise.

"Then one day I thought about my own life, its spiritual high points, and its low points. I correlated these peaks and valleys with measurable quantitative factors relevant to my life—things such as health, wealth, education, career, family, and other socio-economic variables. Amongst all of the individuals still on the list, I asked the Unitronic Database to identify those who seemed to have traits equal and opposite of mine. Assuming there would be room for statistical error, I wasn't surprised there were a dozen possibilities identified. I studied each in detail, ruling them out one by one for various reasons until only your name remained.

"You were raised in a well-to-do family. I was raised in poverty. You were sent to the finest schools. I taught myself to read and write. While you were at the pinnacle of your career, I was scouring the gutters for scraps of food. Now I've reclaimed my life and am blessed with more abundance than I've ever known. You are caught in a downward spiral of growing despair.

"You are my counterpart. I am convinced because I have studied your life and found it to be a perfect match," she said confidently. "The pieces all fit together. It's just that you refuse to admit it to yourself."

"That isn't proof! I've never heard such mumbo jumbo in all my days!"

Vella felt exhausted. She got up and walked over to the narrow window carved out of solid stone and looked upward. "The galaxy's spiral arms are particularly stunning this evening."

Trallix commented, "Oh, come now, my dear sister. You didn't travel five hundred light years from Vatican Prime to talk to me about the status of the night sky. The Mothersoul Superior is much too conservative with her limited resources."

"You're right," said Vella and she turned around and faced Trallix again. "Let me be more direct in my reason for being here."

Trallix looked pleased with himself. A hint of a smile helped to lift his entire face. *Finally*, he thought, *the truth*.

"There is a second part of the theory," Vella finally admitted. "If one of the two souls in a pair ceases to exist, its counterpart must also cease to exist. It's the Second Theorem of Spiritual Mechanics, more commonly known as the Theorem of Spiritual Conservation."

"Don't tell me. Let me guess," mocked the abbot. "You became aware of my situation. You feared my demise. And since you think we're connected by this invisible bond, if I die, you die, too. That's the real reason you're here, isn't it?"

"Yes." Tears silently started to roll down the woman's shallow cheeks. "Is it so wrong to want to live out a full life? Think of it, Trallix. We're only thirty-seven years old and already you're a bitter old man ready to give up on life."

"And you want to keep on living. I knew there had to be some selfish motivation for your visit. No one else gives a damn about me."

"I care about you. Any peace and serenity I claim today has come at the expense of whatever pain you've been through and vice versa. Forgive me, Father, but you can't die. I won't let you. I came to offer you something, anything that would change your mind—something that would give you a reason to live."

"Then you do have a challenge, don't you, my good lady?"

"It's more than just me, Father. You were quite correct when you surmised the Mothersoul Superior wouldn't send me halfway across the sector just to engage in some sort of spiritual wild goose chase."

Trallix seemed even more pleased with himself. "So she's got an interest in this, as well? What's her angle?"

"Ever since the loss of the settlement on Solus II, the

Mothersoul Superior has been very despondent. She has lost faith in the Eternal Oversoul. When she heard my theories, she saw it as a chance to help herself somehow."

"Have you found her spiritual counterpart yet?"

"No. It's one thing for me to have found you. Part of my success is because I knew the intimate details of one of the two souls so well—my own. But with another person, it's hard for me to determine the exact times of the Mothersoul Superior's spiritual highs and lows, making it difficult to whittle down the list of possibilities. And if the theories are erroneous, why waste the time? Proving the theories with the only identifiable set of candidates seemed like a much higher priority."

"What a turn of events. The person responsible for sending me to this desolate piece of rock to contemplate the mysteries of the Eternal Oversoul is now at my mercy!" Trallix grinned. "I can only imagine the Good Mothersoul's face when she realizes that I may have helped to save her life—"

"But you will only get that opportunity if I'm right, mind you. If I'm wrong, whether you live or die, it doesn't affect my life, the life of Mother Superior Aarthra, or her spiritual counterpart one way or the other. However, if I'm right, and I convince you to go on living, I save my own life and the Mothersoul Superior might get a big return on her investment. And if I'm right, and you die before your time, then I die. And you'll never have a chance to gloat. Not a lot of great options, eh?"

"What can you possibly do to bring us more into balance?"

Vella stepped away from the window and returned to where Trallix sat. She stopped at her chair but did not sit down. She inserted her right hand underneath her habit and rummaged around. When she pulled her hand back out, it held a laze-gun.

Trallix blurted out, "Now, wait a minute!"

"You must understand this is the only way."

Trallix's voice started to quiver. "Why did you come here and invade my solitude?" Then, more strongly, "And why are you armed?"

Vella stood silently, her fingers nervously gripping the weapon. Trallix wondered where a nun would find a laze-gun and how she had learned to use it.

The monk spoke again. "What do you really want?"

Vella answered, "I want to help you."

"With a laze-gun in your hand? You have a very strange sense of humor. And your social obligations toward your host are sorely lacking."

"It's not meant to be funny. And I don't care about etiquette. I'm here to save your life—and mine."

"That would be a matter of opinion. It seems as though you entered this sanctuary under false pretenses."

"Perhaps. Perhaps not. I did say your life is in danger."

"That you did, my child. But I certainly didn't think it's because you came to kill me!"

"I'm not interested in killing you—or even hurting you." Vella circled around to corner Trallix. "It is not my time yet. Therefore, it is not yours. You cannot pass on without my accompaniment."

"Are you crazy?"

"No. I'm quite sane, I assure you. You don't seem to understand. I can't let you go on as you're going. If I leave here without doing anything, you will dismiss my warning as pure flight of fancy. You will continue on your spiritual and emotional decline until one day you either die or you commit suicide. At the instant of your death, I, too, will die.

"I need to do something. If I can't stop your descent, then I'll stop my own ascent. I'm going to do something that will upset my success. The Theorem of Spiritual Conservation demands that any harm coming to me be offset with your return to spiritual wholeness. Given a choice between dying a saint or living as a sinner, I'll take the latter."

"And you think harming me will guarantee your survival? I hope you realize what will happen to you if you pull that trigger."

"I am not here to harm you," insisted Sister Vella as she slowly raised her left hand before her and closed all of her fingers around her thumb—all except her small fifth finger. She stepped back and waited for a moment. And then, without expression, she raised the laze-gun and fired at the end of her exposed finger. A bright burst of orange fire shot across the room and the distal phalanx of her finger disappeared. A red stain dripped down her left hand. Vella dropped the laze-gun to the floor. She stared at her right hand in disgust as her face twisted in pain.

The blast hit the wall to the right of Trallix. His effort to dodge the beam caused him to fall off his stool. He slumped against the wall, grabbed at his chest, and tried to catch his breath. He certainly had not expected this outcome.

Across the room, Vella steadied herself. She looked firmly into Trallix's eyes. Her mouth was dry and she found it difficult to talk, but she felt compelled to convince Trallix one last time.

"What I said is the truth. The church has ignored the theories for centuries. No one wants to acknowledge them because it goes against seven thousand years of doctrine."

Trallix reached for his personal communicator with his left hand and punched a series of numbers into it as best he could.

"That's good. Call for help. You'll be fine, you know," said Vella, trying to sound reassuring. Her forehead was damp and she could feel perspiration running down her back again. "I'll take my leave now while I still can get out of this wretched place. I'm sure I will never see you again."

Trembling, she quickly turned away, hiding her eyes from Trallix's stare until she was out of the chamber and heard the heavy door close behind her.

Tears streamed down her face as she fled down the spiral stairway to the front entrance. She whispered to herself, "Please, Eternal Oversoul, forgive me."

"A false balance is an abomination to the LORD:
but a just weight is His delight.
When pride cometh, then cometh shame:
but with the lowly is wisdom.
The integrity of the upright shall guide them:
but the perverseness of transgressors shall destroy them."

PROVERBS 11:1

OF THE GREEN
AND OF THE GOLD

(The Scholar)

············

JARKA MOOSHA WAS AN exosociologist. There were not many experts in this rather eclectic field of study. In fact, there were not many exosociologists at all. There was no reason for there to be—that is, up until ten years ago, nearly a century after lightships were first designed, faster-than-light travel made possible, and the discovery of dozens of worlds resembling Earth in one way or another. What a shock to mankind when evidence of an intelligent extra-terrestrial civilization was found on Aurillia, a small planet orbiting Lalande 21185, a Type M red dwarf star 8.3 light years from Earth. Once all of the excitement died down, all sorts of scientists clamored to be the first to study this or that about the new world and its very unique life forms.

Jarka was one of the lucky ones chosen to be on this, the third, expedition to Aurillia. He would have many long months aboard a rather confining starship with no place to go and little else to do but prepare for this opportunity. Exosociology focused on how alien life forms behaved in their extraterrestrial society, and Jarka planned to make himself as familiar with Aurillia and its inhabitants as possible. How did they interact, cooperate, govern, fight, and view one another? What were their religious beliefs, their attitudes, their instincts, their emotions? And what were their different races, genders, and socio-economic classes?

His initial findings fascinated him. According to the early reports submitted by the first two missions, all of the Aurillians were nearly identical in appearance. Sure, there was a degree of differentiation in size one would assume as a result of age. But aside from that, they were thought to be the same in all significant aspects. There were no obvious morphological differences. It was not yet known whether there were any major physiological differences. Very little work had been done on the biology of the Aurillian body. They all had the same bald head. All wore the same type of plain garment. In fact, the only difference immediately apparent to the first explorers from Earth was that roughly half of the Aurillians wore garments of a green color and the other half wore garments of a gold color. Those dressed in green had a small green triangle on their forehead and were referred to as "Of The Green." Those dressed in gold had a small golden circle on their forehead and were referred to as "Of The Gold."

Jarka found all of this both incredibly interesting from an academic point of view and also very odd. That a society should have so few differences was contrary to everything anyone from Earth who studied the subject of sociology would have expected. Earth's vast numbers of societies were layered with multiple differentiations—variations in gender, race, religion, education, social status, and economic background, to name only the most prominent. On Aurillia, things appeared amazingly simple. An individual's place in the Aurillian society was determined through some unknown practice or custom. One would simply bare the distinction of being Of The Green or Of The Gold. This single characteristic, while perhaps insignificant by Earth standards, might just affect an Aurillian's future life more than anything else.

But as far as Jarka could tell, there were no ramifications from being born into one Aurillian "Color" or the other. Evidently, there were no functions associated with a certain Color and no jobs strictly performed by one Of The Green or Of The Gold. Specialization was apparently driven by some factor or factors Jarka did not understand.

After traveling eight-plus light years, Aurillia now filled his visi-port. Parts of it looked like what the Earth had looked like from orbit when he left so many months ago. Jarka watched intensely as the disk grew larger by the hour. Both planets appeared similar from space, which would be expected if both worlds were habitable and comfortably suited to support intelligent life. There were cloud patterns, desert areas, hemispheres of day and night, and the same clusters of artificial lights sprinkled across the night hemisphere. Glimpses of Aurillia's surface came and went through the clouds. Because he did not have sufficient knowledge of Aurillian geography, the coastlines were not familiar to him. He had the strong sense Aurillia was rotating quickly beneath him, but he realized it was the lightship spiraling downward. The ship must be in its final stages of approach, he thought.

Jarka could hear the noises associated with preparations for landing occurring beneath him. He knew nothing of the latest model lightship, its size, its crew complement, or what made it work. He only knew he would be glad to have feet firmly planted on solid ground, even if it was on alien ground.

His thoughts turned to the Sree Airia who would greet him and serve as his sponsor while on Aurillia. The scant knowledge on Aurillian social structure suggested that a *sree* was a pair of individuals, one Of The Green and one Of The Gold, who served together in some capacity of government, industry, or education. But what made the *sree* an interesting social unit was, once formed, the two individuals worked together in both the home and the workplace. They rarely left one another's side. Jarka tried to imagine Earth marriages if man and wife didn't receive a periodic break from one another's company!

The Sree Airia consisted of Matan—Of The Gold—and Palan—Of The Green. Their particular role was the Director—or more appropriately Directors—of the Institute of Sociological Studies for ExtraStellars. Unlike Earth, though, disciplines relating to extraterrestrial intelligence were well established on Aurillia. Jarka wondered why this was so.

The Institute had granted Jarka's request—or more accurately the request of Earth's International Association of Exosociology—for access to material on Aurillian society and interviews with a cross section of Aurillians. Permission had been granted to interview twelve individuals during the three-week stay on the surface of Aurillia. The way Jarka figured it, he would be interviewing someone about every other day. That would leave him time to study the various media made available to him, as well as time for some mingling with Aurillians in their natural habitat.

Once the starship touched down in the middle of a large paved area resembling an Earth airport, Jarka began to review in his mind everything he knew about the physical appearance of Aurillians. The first explorers described the adults as being somewhat shorter than humans, perhaps a bit more slender, and possessing pale tan skin. They had two arms and two legs, and their heads were slightly larger by Earth standards, likely the result of well-developed brains. A small nose was located midway between their eyes and their mouth. Not too terribly different from human beings, considering the odds against an extraterrestrial race having even the faintest resemblance to humans, thought Jarka.

What might the Aurillians think about his physical form? To them, Jarka would most certainly appear tall, although his height of 1.8 meters was about average for the male crew members of the expedition. His broad shoulders and lean physique gave him an appearance of strength, though Jarka had no obvious muscles. He possessed a face framed with a short neatly trimmed beard. This served to give him an air of intelligence, especially in academic circles. His hair, as well as his beard, was dirty blond with a trace of gray at the temples. A long nose, both rugged and pleasant, served as the center of Jarka's face—a perfect match for his warm and inviting personality. How the Aurillians would perceive these alien features, Jarka didn't know.

After several hours of what Jarka presumed to be necessary maintenance and systems checks, the hatch opened and a short stairway protruded from the belly of the lightship. A contingency of about fifty individuals ventured out. Representatives from all parts of the mission, as well as a collection of the principal investigators—including Jarka—were the fortunate ones chosen for this privilege.

A delegation of several hundred Aurillians gathered shortly after touchdown, patiently waiting for the travelers from Earth to disembark. A mixture of green and gold forms sat half a kilometer or so from the port side of the ship. Quite a contrast to the contagious excitement sweeping over the crew from Earth.

As Jarka stepped out of the sleek hull and onto the tarmac, he remembered having read reports of expeditions to some of the other planets mankind had touched in its quest to find another intelligent species. They said each world had its own unique odor. Aurillia was no exception. But rather than having a pungent or acidic aroma to it, the air had a very sweet scent, almost one of light perfume.

And what his nose found pleasant, his eyes found soothing. From the washed-out blue sky—faint by Earth standards—to the scarlet leaves on the abundant vegetation, to the soft edges on all of the buildings, Aurillia's appearance did little to offend Jarka's senses. He found the whole experience entirely pleasing as he walked toward his first encounter with the Aurillians.

After an hour and a half of speeches and formal ceremonies, Jarka worked his way through the crowd of dignitaries and introduced himself to Matan and Palan. The reports had been right, thought Jarka. It was difficult to discern an Aurillian Of One Color from another Aurillian Of The Same Color. But the few Aurillians Jarka approached and mistakenly thought to be his contacts didn't seem to mind the error and politely pointed the Earthman in the right direction.

"I am very appreciative that your Institute has been so cooperative in giving me a free hand to study Aurillian society," said Jarka as he bowed slightly to Matan and Palan in Aurillian custom. "If I am to understand our agreement correctly, you have granted me twelve interviews with individuals from all walks of Aurillian life, as well as access to the Institute's library."

"That is correct," replied Palan.

"Tell me, Directors, if it is at all possible, might I be able to experience your society firsthand—you know, by taking walks and mingling with citizens on the street?"

Jarka's keen powers of observation did not miss the fact his question caused a distinct change on Matan's face. In fact, the Aurillian's entire head seemed to change shape momentarily. Whereas the features on a human face change with different emotions, the shape of an Aurillian's head can change, shifting from its usual oval shape to a slightly more spherical appearance—presumably in response to different emotions. Had Jarka better understood the subtleties of their peculiar facial shapes, he might have been able to discern what emotion Matan was not sharing. But Jarka got the distinct impression his presence was not entirely welcome. Perhaps something was being hidden, thought Jarka—and he wanted to find out what.

"Yes, of course—you may go out into our society and speak with those you encounter," answered Matan finally. Jarka imagined Matan wished to add the phrase "—just don't find anything." Matan continued, "Please do not forget your obligation to our agreement, though. We wish to review your observations and your findings before you leave us."

"I look forward to it," responded Jarka. "Until then?" Jarka waited for an instant to see whether either of the Directors had any additional remarks. Sensing their business concluded, he bowed slightly again and turned to find his way back to the lightship.

The next morning an escort met Jarka on the tarmac and transported him to a rather spacious room at the Institute. It would serve as Jarka's home away from home. He would conduct all of his interviews there. Many large tables filled the room. Jarka selected one of them for his desk. No sooner did Jarka unpack his portable computer interface and a recording device from a lightweight metallic briefcase than his first interviewee arrived, escorted by one of Matan's many subordinates.

"Good morning. My name is Jarka Moosha of Planet Earth. I will be asking you some questions and you simply respond by speaking into the electro-phone," he said, pointing in the direction of the small metallic cylinder at the end of a flex arm.

"Could you please state your name?"

"Sarillion."

"Okay. Thank you, Sarillion. You know, I am very curious about the fact that everyone in your society is evidently identical—except, of course, for the difference in Color. I wonder if you could tell me a little bit about how this originated."

"Certainly. Several thousand cycles ago, we did not have the Colors. We were a people divided by our many differences. These differences caused us to harbor great jealousy of one another. Our jealousy gave birth to anger, and our anger caused us to wage war and kill one another. After a thousand cycles of killing, there were few of our people left.

"It was then that a very brave Aurillian priest went to our world's most sacred temple. He fasted and prayed for twenty-seven rotations. On the night of the twenty-seventh rotation, two faces appeared in the midst of the burning incense.

"'We are the Supreme Sree,' said the faces in unison. 'We hear your summons.'

"The young priest was a bit confused. You see, up until that time in our history, our Deity was thought to be a single entity. For there to be two faces was quite a shock.

"The priest then verbalized his prayers. 'Your Holinesses, our people have fought and killed one another almost to the point of extinction. I come seeking a better way of life for us. I ask that you remove all of our differences and, therefore, our incentive to fight and to kill.'

"'We hear your prayer and will grant your request. Listen closely, for you must bear our message to your people,' said the Sree.

"The rest of the night was spent with the Supreme Deities dictating to the priest all he must do. The priest faithfully wrote down everything, stopping the Sree only to question points unclear to him.

"As the first rays of morning light entered the Sacred Place, the mists faded along with the faces of the Supreme Sree. The priest returned to his people and began to explain to them everything they must do.

"The priest first taught the people about the *eglanti*, the shapes you see on our foreheads today. He instructed them how to make the icons by adding certain extracts from Aurillian flowers and plants to various minerals in just the right proportions to produce the powerful talismans of change. You see, each *eglanti* removes all desire to be different once it touches the forehead of a newborn Aurillian. He also made certain they understood they were always to make an equal number of green and gold *eglanti*, as half of the people would wear the Green Triangle and half would wear the Gold Circle.

"The priest then introduced the *tholcon* to the people—the gown you see us wear—and explained that half of them would dress in Green and half would dress in Gold, to match their *eglanti*. These differences in garments and Colors would serve as a reminder of our shameful past, full of war and hatred, and of how the Supreme Sree brought peace to our planet.

"Next, he explained the concept of the *sree* and how individuals would pair off—one Of The Green with one Of The Gold. This joining of One Color with the Other Color would prevent this last remaining difference in our world from being a spark for more war and killing. The Supreme Deities—through the introduction of the *eglanti*, the *tholcon*, and the *sree*—removed all anger from our planet. The priest emphasized repeatedly the need to honor the sanctity of the *eglanti*, the *tholcon*, and the *sree*—and how any deviation from these practices would bring swift and certain death.

"Lastly, the priest made all the people understand that in doing these things, they would be following the example of their Supreme Power. It was then he revealed to them the true nature of their Deity—that they, too, wore the Green and the Gold.

"The people were so tired of killing and war that they accepted everything the priest taught them. Our entire society transformed, our people multiplied, and our world rebuilt."

"And your world has lasted as such since then?" inquired Jarka.

"Yes."

"The sanctity of the *eglanti*, the *tholcon*, and the *sree* has been maintained?"

"To the best of my knowledge," replied Sarillion.

"Thank you for that," said Jarka. He flipped through his notepad, searching for the next set of questions.

Later that same day, Jarka spoke with Larinda, a prominent scientist. Jarka asked questions ranging from the level of technological advances and its effect on society to the moral and ethical dilemmas created by such breakthroughs—not the least of which being contact with Earth. Jarka wound up the second session discussing rank and privilege on Aurillia.

"Do all individuals in Aurillian society have the same rights and privileges, regardless of Color?"

"Yes."

"Do all have equal access to education?"

"Yes."

Jarka wanted something more than the short polite responses given by Larinda. *Politeness and properness are all well and good*, he thought, *but they don't fill blank pages of academic journals.* He switched tactics and began asking open-ended questions. Jarka made a mental note to enroll in a class on interview techniques when he returned to Earth.

"Why?" Jarka looked at his interviewee with a very satisfied grin. He let several moments of silence pass.

"If there were some advantage to being Of One Color or another, then our society would fall apart. There must be equal numbers of the Colors to assure the survival of both Of The Colors."

Okay, Jarka said to himself. *If it worked once, maybe it will work again.*

"Why?"

"A very delicate balance is maintained between the Colors. It is absolutely essential for our society. The designation of one's Color has been left to our Higher Powers, not those raising our young."

The following afternoon, Jarka interviewed Valirra—an administrative assistant in a government records office. The session began with routine questions about government but soon turned to other areas of interest.

"Valirra? What sort of name might that be?" Jarka had not been able to discern any clue within the Aurillian pool of names he could use as a tool in guessing whether a particular name belonged to someone Of The Green or someone Of The Gold. On Earth, most languages assigned certain types of words as being masculine or feminine. Earth names were likewise predisposed to one gender or the other, allowing one to guess with a high degree of certainty that a name belonged to a man or a woman.

"From the name alone I can't be certain whether one would be Of The Green or Of The Gold," he continued. "Perhaps you might explain to me if there is any connection."

"There is no connection," observed Valirra. "Although, I am sometimes taken to be Of The Gold by those who have never met me."

"Why would they think that?" said Jarka, pondering how these strange folks could derive any association between "Color" and name.

"Judging from my name, they are justified. I'm told Valirra is a popular name for individuals Of The Gold in outlying provinces."

"I've not encountered the name in my reading. Not that I'm any great expert on Aurillian names."

"That's because you have not traveled much on Aurillia."

"So there is no relationship between your name and your Color?"

"Precisely."

"How do you choose a name for a young Aurillian?" inquired Jarka.

Valirra began to recite the lengthy process for choosing a name, quoting verses from some ancient Aurillian text. Jarka could not have been happier as he scribbled furiously on his notepad and fed more blank cartridges into the tape machine.

After a short break, Dedra entered the room shyly, almost on tiptoe, wearing a soft velvety green *tholcon*, uniquely decorated by a subtle pattern of fine dark emerald webbing. The *tholcon* was not entirely unattractive, but it was certainly efficient at covering up any noticeable physical differences between the Colors. Dedra's belt was wider than Valirra's and was a slightly different shade of green.

Aurillians did manage to decorate themselves even within their rather minimal fashion parameters. Jarka hoped he could learn more about the *tholcon* as Dedra was the owner of a small shop in the city—reportedly makers of the finest garments on all of Aurillia.

"Are there any differences in the clothes worn by those Of The Green and those Of The Gold?" began Jarka.

"The *tholcons* worn by all of those Of The Gold are nearly identical with the *tholcons* worn by all of those Of The Green—except the Color, of course. There are slight variations depending on region and personal tastes. But they are subtle and may not be noticeable to the untrained eye." Dedra seemed to point to certain parts of the *tholcon*. Jarka looked at the *tholcon* from across the table without being blatant about it and could see hints of shapes in the weave.

"And what about underneath the *tholcon*? What do you wear under your *tholcons*?" continued Jarka.

"We wear additional garments underneath our *tholcons*," answered Dedra.

"Are these undergarments colored? Do they match the Color of the outer garment?"

"Yes."

Jarka decided to push his luck with one more question about this potentially embarrassing subject matter. "Are there any differences between the undergarments of one Color and the other?"

Dedra's face took on what Jarka believed to be a puzzled look. Dedra responded slowly by simply stating, "No."

—— o0o ——

Jarka looked forward to his time with Mallara. Mallara performed a function Jarka understood to be roughly equivalent to that of a nurse. When he met Mallara, he somehow expected Mallara to be wearing a white uniform with a red cross prominently displayed somewhere on the front left pocket. But this being Aurillia, Mallara's golden *tholcon* was all there was.

"Is a *sree* always made up of one individual Of The Green and one individual Of The Gold?"

"Yes."

"And never two individuals Of The Green or two individuals Of The Gold," Jarka continued.

"No. Such things simply do not occur," stated Mallara with an almost anxious look.

While Jarka was curious about the mating rituals of Aurillia, he was even more eager to know how the Aurillians reproduced. Since he had not been directed by any official to stay away from certain subjects, he thought it would be safe to inquire about this topic.

"How do the people of Aurillia reproduce?" Jarka asked Mallara. "Do individuals who are Of The Green interact in some manner or another with individuals Of The Gold to produce an offspring?"

"Yes," answered Mallara. "One member of the *sree* serves as One Who Carries and the other member of the *sree* serves as One Who Does Not Carry. The One Who Does Not Carry transfers genetic material to the One Who Carries and the gestation period begins."

Jarka scratched his head for a minute. *So there is another differentiation in their society? Those Who Carry and Those Who Do Not Carry*, he thought. He went back to questioning Mallara.

"Tell me, is there any relationship between individuals Of The Gold and Those Who Carry or Those Who Do Not Carry?"

"No. An individual of either Color can serve as One Who Carries." Mallara returned to silently staring at some point on the other side of the room.

Jarka was again thwarted in his quest to find some basis for the differentiation between the Colors. If Aurillians Who Carry equated to Earth females and Aurillians Who Do Not Carry equated to Earth males, then a model making some sense might be constructed. Likewise, if Aurillians who were Of The Green equated to Earth males and Aurillians who were Of The Gold equated to Earth females, that, too, might make sense. But so far, Jarka could not come to any such conclusion.

He decided to take another approach. Since he assumed all Aurillians appeared the same without their *tholcons* on, how would new parents know whether their "newborn," if that was the correct term, would be Of The Green or Of The Gold?

"After a new Aurillian is born, how do you know which Color is appropriate?"

"Ahhhh—that is one of our most sacred mysteries."

Jarka allowed a very long pregnant pause, hoping Mallara's response would continue, but it did not.

"Please describe the process, if you don't mind, and we need not concern ourselves with the mystery part," rephrased Jarka, "if you don't want to, that is."

"Both Colors of *eglanti* are placed on the forehead of the newborn—first one Color, then the other. Each Color of *eglanti* is left on the forehead for one rotation. Once removed, the correct Color will leave an outline of its shape. That is how one's Color is determined. Why one Color instead of another, no one knows."

"Fascinating," reflected Jarka. "Completely random."

Jarka welcomed his first day in a week with no interviews or appointments scheduled. After spending several hours going through books and files kindly provided to him by the Sree Airia, he decided to go outside and get some "fresh" air, if one could consider the alien air with its perfume-like scents, fresh. More than the chance to get out into the open and exercise his legs, he wanted the opportunity to mingle with the native Aurillians and observe them in their own environment.

Once outside, Jarka looked up at the sky. The clouds seemed to wear a slight pinkish tint—their shade not any more colored than clouds involved in an extraordinary sunset on Earth. But the open sky was not nearly as blue as one would see on the clearest of days back home. Light pink on light blue. It struck Jarka that the Universe might be playing some sort of ironic joke on him as he struggled to understand how the Aurillians segregated themselves in the fashion they did and the basis for it.

He headed down the street to his left and began to inspect the skyline. Whereas on Earth, all of the buildings in older cities had a square or rectangular cross section with a flat roof, the structures here were mostly cylindrical with a hemispherical top. What truly stood out, however, were the spires decorating the buildings, reaching skyward until their pointed tops pricked the washed-out crimson clouds.

As Jarka wandered through what roughly equated to

the downtown section of the city, he noticed an open area he assumed to be a park—the area covered with a short purple ground covering, something resembling grass back on Earth. In the center of the park, a fountain shot water straight up for several meters, forming sphere-like globules, each seeming to float in midair for a moment before dropping back into the pond. The plants consisted of sculpted shrubs and willow-shaped trees, all decorated with varying shades of characteristic purple. Along the paths and around the fountain bloomed *femerod*, the native flowers of every pastel shade imaginable. He also noticed the drone of some very bizarre-looking insects—none of whom, fortunately, were interested in bothering anyone from Earth.

Jarka felt pleased with himself for having found this small patch of familiarity in the midst of an increasingly alien world with all of its differences in colors, shapes, and sizes of the flora and fauna. As he leisurely strolled through the park, following the meandering paved walkways, he saw several other Aurillians taking advantage of the nice weather. He found a large round stone facing the fountain with a slight depression in its center, as though it were made to fit the backside of an Aurillian body. Jarka decided to sit for a few minutes and observe the passersby and clear his thoughts. One individual Of The Gold walked past, looked at him briefly with a stare not characteristic of those with whom he had spoken, then sat down in another stone chair facing Jarka. The Aurillian opened up a book and started to read.

Jarka returned to scanning the park and the adjoining street—and the Aurillian who sat on the opposite side of the fountain. After several minutes, Jarka couldn't help but notice the Aurillian looked up at him again, this time more curiously. Jarka wasn't certain if it was his own alien appearance attracting attention or something else. This individual's manners seemed out of context compared to the overt politeness of the introverted interviewees selected for Jarka to question.

Jarka watched the Aurillian as non-saliently as possible. The alien seemed to be involved in some sort of internal debate. He observed the unique oscillations between a long narrow face and a broad flat face. Jarka thought the elastic nature of Aurillian physiology to be one of the most fascinating features of the species. After several minutes, it looked as though this Aurillian wanted to speak, then seemed to think better of it, then seemed to want to speak again. Jarka waited patiently for the resolution.

Not surprisingly, this particular Aurillian appeared the same as all of the other Aurillians—all features not covered by the *tholcon* completely without any distinguishing characteristics. But one way or another, Jarka became convinced there was something very different about this individual. It was the look of fear, he finally decided. This Aurillian definitely looked nervous and seemed afraid. What the source of the fear was, Jarka didn't have a clue.

Finally, the hesitant Aurillian got up and walked the short distance over to Jarka's seat and stopped directly in front of the exosociologist. "Excuse me, but aren't you Jarka Moosha from Planet Earth—the one here to study our society?"

"Why, yes I am," said Jarka, relieved the Aurillian's internal struggle appeared to be over and excited about an unscheduled interview.

"May I speak with you?" Before Jarka could respond, the Aurillian asked a second question. "Would you mind if we walked while we talked?" The stranger backed away slightly as if to encourage Jarka to stand up.

"Certainly. We can walk," said a surprised but agreeable Jarka, perplexed because this Aurillian exhibited a forwardness not yet seen by Jarka during his interviews. "How may I be of assistance to you?"

"I know you have come a very long distance to learn about Aurillia and how we interact as a society. I know you have been granted twelve interviews during your stay. My fear is that the Institute arranged the individuals whom you are to interview such that you would not be exposed to one seemingly small, but very critical, facet in our culture.

"Jarka Moosha, it is very important to me you take me seriously. I am risking my life even by being seen with you, let alone speaking with you. In an effort to demonstrate to you just how serious what I have to say to you is, I am going to tell you my name."

"That is really not necessary," said Jarka.

"No, it is something I must do," continued the nervous Aurillian. "My name is Casla. Actually—Caslarian Of The Sree Rian." And without any further hesitation, Casla got directly to the point. Jarka sensed an urgency in the Aurillian's high-pitched voice and fear in his repeated glances at the fellow pedestrians in the surrounding park.

"There are Aurillians who are born Of One Color who have unexplainable desires to be Of The Other Color. I am one such individual. We who have this . . . inclination, for lack of a better word, have learned to conceal it. To be suspected of having this inclination is horrible. If an individual is proven to have the inclination—by whatever methodology or circumstance—it means death for the individual."

"What? Are you sure?" Jarka questioned. This information, to his knowledge, had not been included in the mission reports of the previous two expeditions to Aurillia. *Maybe this is what Matan and Palan did not want me to find.* "I thought your society abhorred violence," he added.

"It does. But Aurillia does not view the death of someone with this inclination as violence. It views it as survival—an obligation to the Supreme Sree, a necessary action to keep the world free of the evils from our past, a sort of cleansing to keep our society pure."

Casla went on in a manner very uncharacteristic for an Aurillian. "Rumors of color-crossing run through our society. Though color-crossing is rare, it does exist. It has erroneously come to connote illness, mistrust, and evil. Its existence is even denied by the very individuals who are inflicted by its forceful presence. Our society is filled with moral critics who, by insisting on the horror of color-crossing, have planted a strong distaste in every member of Aurillian society. They have taken something not harmful and created an impenetrable barrier between the Colors. The true victims of color-crossing are not the countless millions in our otherwise pristine masses, but rather those who must struggle daily with its curse on the inside and the discrimination waged against our kind on the outside.

"Color-crossing in its simplest form is nothing more than making a choice for ourselves, reversing a choice made for us when we were born, without the chance to come to know ourselves or speak for ourselves. Those who upon reaching the age of maturity and make a decision to follow their feelings, do so with the disapproval of others. I believe other Aurillians are jealous of those who make such a choice, jealous of the courage to feel what might be inside and to act on those feelings."

"Does anyone else know of your inclination?" inquired Jarka a bit hesitantly.

"The One With Whom I Share is not aware of this thing," responded Casla. There were several moments of silence. They continued to walk through the now almost empty park.

Casla continued. "But I have a friend named Asdra, one Of The Green, whom I have known for many cycles. Recently, I sought out Asdra because the One With Whom I Share has become increasingly distant. I had developed a need to share knowledge of my inclination with someone. I came to feel I could not bear the burden of it alone any longer. I learned to trust Asdra. One night, I took a risk and told Asdra of it. Asdra understood. We often share time together, discuss this thing, and there is comfort. To my surprise, Asdra told me of a sibling who is Of The Green and wishes to be Of The Gold."

"Have you ever changed your appearance—I mean on a temporary basis—such that you follow through on your inclination and present the image of one who is Of The Green?" Only the constant hum of insects followed the question.

Casla finally nodded in an affirmative motion and whispered, "Yes—I am embarrassed to admit this. Every cell in my body is filled with shame." A look of intense pain crossed Casla's face.

"When I heard a sociologist from Earth was to visit our planet, I knew I must contact you and make you aware of our plight," Casla said with a renewed sense of urgency. "I was certain all of your arranged interviewees would be instructed to avoid any mention of individuals such as myself."

"You are very right about that, my new friend," comforted Jarka.

"You must find a way to raise this issue with Matan and Palan and beg them to understand. Likewise, you must tell Earth. Perhaps your planet might be able to bring some pressure to bear on our government to stop killing those of my kind."

Nearly half an hour had passed since Casla started talking to Jarka and already he felt a special closeness to this courageous individual. He wasn't certain he understood the concept of color-crossing entirely, but he knew of similar things on Earth. But he was more concerned about Casla's safety. Though grateful for the piece of knowledge Casla gave him, he did not want that gain to come at the expense of Casla's life.

Jarka sensed something had changed in his Aurillian companion; perhaps Casla felt some relief—some peace. Jarka knew this issue could not remain buried here on Aurillia. But he also knew this planet would not easily allow news of color-crossing to find its way to Earth. Earth was the key.

"Casla," started Jarka, "you have risked much today. I appreciate what you have done. I will respect your privacy and I will deliver your message. You have my word. Now, please, for your own safety, go back to your business and take good care of yourself."

"Thank you very much, Jarka Moosha. You have given me hope." Casla excused himself, headed off toward a grove of tall bush-like plants, and disappeared.

On his walk back to his small quarters aboard the lightship, Jarka couldn't help thinking about Casla and his revelation about Aurillian society. As he mulled things over in his mind, his eyes scanned the streets, observing all combinations of Colors walking and doing things together. It struck him that he never saw any public displays of affection—no one holding hands, or hugging, or kissing. Everyone treated each other in a polite, courteous, almost professional manner.

Jarka slept uneasily that night. Thoughts of Casla continued to echo in his mind. The most chilling thought that kept coming back to him was the existence of a death penalty for an act so simple in a society so peaceful. On several occasions, he awoke, his mind trying to fit the pieces together, only to fall back asleep.

In the days following Jarka's chance meeting with Casla, he conducted a series of interviews with Aurillians whose names were as strange as everyone else's to whom he had talked. Donora was Of The Gold and a journalist, Irillia was Of The Green and taught young Aurillians, and Quora was also Of The Green and worked on a farm growing different food crops. Gathalla and Gawnalla—that is to say, the Sree Alla—were Of The Green and Of The Gold respectively, and served as copresidents of a small company that manufactured parts for automated transport devices.

All of these interviews paled in comparison to the walk with Casla. These exchanges with Aurillians from across the social spectrum proved to be interesting enough and would certainly serve to deepen Earth's understanding of the inner workings of Aurillia. But the subject of color-crossing would not leave Jarka's mind. He found himself eagerly anticipating the end of this second round of questioning. As he wrapped up his interview with Gathalla and Gawnalla, he neatly placed his notes and small recording device in his briefcase and headed for the library wing of the main Institute building. He no longer required an escort, having learned his way around the grounds.

Jarka's academic curiosity about this thing causing so much fear in Casla continued to grow. Surely, the psychology journals of this world would examine color-crossing. Maybe they might document the most current theories on the origin of color-crossing and debate whether it was a physiological condition or an emotional illness.

Jarka spent the next four hours in the Institute's library. He asked the librarians where he might find more information on color-crossing. They handed him journals and textbooks and video microtapes, but none of the employees would answer any questions about color-crossing. He soon realized there was no use in asking anyone else. None of the Aurillians wanted to have anything to do with the subject or even anyone interested in the subject. All seemed very uncomfortable if it was so much as mentioned.

When he was finished, he knew this much—Casla had been right. Color-crossing was treated as a perversion and anyone thought to be a victim of it was mistrusted and shunned until they were either exonerated or tried as a criminal and killed. Of paramount interest to Jarka was the complete absence of any cause for the syndrome. Evidently, no one knew the origin of the condition. Maybe the uncertainty was what they feared.

—— o0o ——

At noon the following day, Jarka was back at his desk, preparing for his session with Maeda. He finally decided on a more direct approach in his quest for information on what he had come to refer to as transcoloration—or what Casla had called color-crossing.

"What is the most serious crime in Aurillian society?" Jarka asked.

A look resembling disgust crossed the face of Maeda, a well-respected judge, one Of The Gold, and someone, by Jarka's estimation, likely to be older than the other Aurillians he had encountered.

"The violation of our most sacred taboo. No one who is Of The Green must ever seek to be Of The Gold. The opposite is just as forbidden." Maeda offered no additional words of explanation.

"Could you explain to me something, anything, about this phenomena?"

"There are those born to one Color or the other who desire to change their Color. This is forbidden."

"Yes, I know it is forbidden, but why?"

"One who is Of One Color casts his life aside and steals life away from The Other Color when they think about, or talk about, or take any action having anything to do with efforts to become one Of The Other Color. There is no greater crime."

"What is the punishment for such a crime?"

"Death. Justice is served quickly and fairly." After a brief moment, Maeda reiterated the word "Death."

"Are there other crimes considered to be as serious?"

"Only one. Anyone who is Of One Color cannot enter into a *sree* with one Of The Same Color. That is also strictly forbidden."

"And what is the punishment for that?"

"The same—death."

Jarka let several moments go by before he started addressing a different topic. "Tell me something about your religious beliefs. Who is the Supreme Sree? What are the cornerstones of your religion? Do you believe in an afterlife?"

Maeda answered each question in great detail, not revealing anything Jarka did not already know.

Jarka then asked a question in hopes of setting a trap. "Your religious beliefs hold that all life is sacred, do they not?"

"That is true," replied Maeda.

"And that it is wrong for one to take the life of another?"

"Yes, we believe that."

"You just told me your most serious crimes brought with them a death penalty. Doesn't this conflict with your decree that no living being should kill another living being?"

"One who is Of One Color and wishes to be Of The Other Color is mocking the Supreme Sree. We cannot love those who have so much disdain for the Supreme Sree. Those who violate our most sacred commandment must be sent to the Supreme Sree for judgment. Only the Supreme Sree can have compassion for those affected." Jarka constantly marveled at the Aurillians unending ability to sit perfectly still while talking—no gesturing with one's hands, no apparent body language, only subtle distortions to the shape of the heads and their faces as they revealed brief flashes of emotion.

"So you see no contradiction in putting to death those who color-cross?"

"I do not have an opinion on this issue. I merely believe in the sanctity of the Supreme Sree. Their commands must be met—regardless of the cost."

Jarka dismissed his interviewee, still not convinced Aurillia had fully thought through the moral paradox brought by their choice of solutions of dealing with color-crossing. He left the room for the evening, shaking his head and muttering to himself.

The day came for Jarka's last two interviews during his stay on Aurillia. One of Matan's escorts quite unexpectedly met him outside the lightship and informed him the final interviews would be with Matan and Palan. While this puzzled Jarka, he did feel fortunate to be able to spend a little time questioning the Sree Airia.

Upon arriving at the Directors' Office, Jarka found both Matan and Palan were sitting very still in what Jarka now knew to be typical Aurillian fashion. Jarka took a moment to unpack his notebooks from his briefcase and organize them on a triangular table in the middle of the room.

When he finished, he stood before them, studying the faces of the Institute's directors. The shadowy gold of their Aurillian skin seemed to have paled and grayed in the two-and-a-half weeks since he had seen them last. Matan and Palan looked Jarka over for what seemed minutes, examining him with their eyes from the top of his head to the tips of his toes. Jarka felt as though their discerning eyes left nothing unnoticed, at least on the outside anyway. After minutes ticked by, he wondered if they weren't also able to see within and were examining some morsel they had found in his thoughts with equal scrutiny.

"Good morning, Sree Airia," Jarka said, smiling. "I am so very pleased to have the opportunity to speak with you. You and your Institute and all of the individuals whom you have allowed me to meet have been very gracious and very informative. I, and my colleagues on Earth who will benefit from this study, greatly appreciate your hospitality."

"You are most welcome," came the short, polite response. But instead of Jarka asking the first question, Matan fired a single short question at the sociologist from Earth.

"Jarka Moosha—you have become aware of color-crossing, have you not?"

A visibly shaken Jarka stared at Matan. "Yes, I have. I am most fascinated by the existence of these individuals who are Of One Color but wish to be Of The Other Color. But how did you know that I—"

"How did we discover that you found out about the blemish in our otherwise perfect society?" interrupted Matan. "We know you were approached by a certain Aurillian. We know because we have been following many color-crossers. And because we have been, how shall you say, keeping our eye on your activities. We know you promised not to pass along the name, but this is information we already knew."

Jarka responded, carefully choosing his words. "It was obvious to me this individual has great fear about what will happen if the presence of the inclination is made known to you. And there are others who share the fear. I am to understand there are many such individuals present in your society. They believe they are born into such feelings to be Of The Other Color. I am also to understand there is a punishment of death keeping most Aurillians with the inclination quiet and separated from others with similar inclinations."

"We have heard the argument that such 'inclinations,' as you call them, are given at the beginning of life. We do not agree. We believe they come when a young Aurillian is brought up in an environment in which the One Who Does Not Carry is absent throughout much of the formative years and the One Who Carries is overbearing and seeks to use the young, rather than an absent mate, to meet their emotional needs. The forces released by such interactions come to bear on the young Aurillian and cause their subconscious mind to form associations that are emotionally unhealthy.

"You have been thorough, Jarka Moosha. It is apparent to us you have succeeded in penetrating to the very core of the Aurillian social fabric. You have found what is sacred to us, what we fear, what we value, and what we find disgusting. Congratulations."

"Thank you. I will accept that as a compliment," Jarka said with a slight bow. "I realize I am a disturbing influence in a tightly knit society such as yours. I bring a different set of criteria with which to evaluate your population."

"We are learning from our experience with those of you from Planet Earth that Aurillians do not like to be evaluated, studied, perhaps ultimately judged, or treated as specimens any more than your world would," said Palan, pointing a finger at Jarka.

"We have our emotions," continued Matan. "Each Aurillian fits into a comfortable niche. The appearance of an alien such as yourself without a fixed color is unsettling to us."

"Your division based on Colors does involve a certain amount of inflexibility," observed Jarka.

"Granted," replied Matan quickly, "but there is also a certain self-assurance that comes from it. We have been given firm rules for our Colors. Each individual knows their place, accepts it, and is accepted in it."

"But I am curious," said Jarka, "why did you not mention this color-crossing earlier? It appears as though you made efforts to hide its presence from me."

"The Institute thought it unnecessary to address this issue with you and your world. And if it had not been for your chance meeting with the color-crosser, you might never have become aware of the existence of such a thing. We felt you need not know or be concerned with it." Matan then added in a quiet voice, "As an Earthman, I suppose you do not understand."

"As a sociologist, I think I do." Jarka thought fleetingly of the taboos on his home planet. There were many that might be as strong.

"We have Casla in custody," said Palan matter-of-factly. Jarka stared at the two directors in disbelief. So he really had been followed during his walk with Casla. His heart immediately sank as he thought of the likely fate awaiting his friend.

Jarka blurted out, "May I speak to Casla?"

"On no account," came the absolute response.

Jarka could feel himself becoming agitated. "Is the presence of color-crossers so harmful? Why can't they be accepted into your society? There is no real difference between them and any other Aurillian!"

Matan said swiftly, "You do not understand, do you?"

"And for this one difference, you will condemn an individual to death?"

"We have no other choice," said Matan. The agony in Matan's voice convinced Jarka of the severity this situation caused the Aurillians. "The Supreme Sree took away our ancient anger with instructions that the integrity of the Colors—the *eglanti*, the *tholcon*, and the *sree*—be maintained. Color-crossing violates that condition and we feel the old anger when we think of it. If color-crossers are not removed, they will give a foothold to an emotion that almost destroyed our planet once. We cannot allow this to happen again."

"This is totally outrageous! You have no right!" shouted Jarka. Jarka's outburst puzzled Matan.

"Is this anger? I have never observed such anger."

"Yes! This is anger!" Jarka's fist slammed onto the table.

"You now can understand our point. The very presence of color-crossing has given anger the opportunity to rise once again its ugly head in our world. We beg of you not to report the existence of color-crossing to your home-world. It is apparent your kind cannot tolerate *our* solution to *our* problem any more than we can tolerate your anger."

"No! I will not honor your request!" declared Jarka. "This cannot be allowed to go on if there is to be a lasting relationship between our two worlds. Mistrust is the fruit of ignorance. If we are to be the masons of mutual friendship, we must be willing to share the totality of our societies, all the good, and the beauty, as well as all of the bad, and the pain."

Jarka stood in front of the table for several moments. He was content to let the Aurillians terminate the interview. Matan stood up, followed by Palan. Jarka bowed slightly before Matan politely motioned the Earthman to head for the triangular door and the waiting escort who had brought him from the lightship.

The evening before the lightship was to lift off for Earth, Jarka did not feel much like working. There would be many long months to process and analyze the information he had collected. His mind could not stop thinking about Casla. Jarka wandered aimlessly through the lightship until he ended up in the communications center. He noticed the young lieutenant on duty had tuned into the Aurillian Evening Holocast.

After a couple of brief news stories, pictures of two Aurillians appeared. Since one was Of The Gold and one was Of The Green, Jarka first thought it was a *sree* being discussed. Then a streak of horror shot through his consciousness. It was Casla! Jarka moved closer to the holo-set so he could hear the story.

"—And today the convicted color-crosser, Casla, and his close friend and accomplice, Asdra, were put to death. The traditional waiting period was ignored due to the severity of their offense. In an official statement released by the government shortly before their execution, the Emperors said color-crossing will not be tolerated. They reinforced the warning that anyone who willingly assists someone who is a known color-crosser will share the death penalty. Such was the case today with the second execution."

Jarka sat stunned—outraged. He lost his breath. Casla and Asdra dead! Was this Aurillian justice? Were the Aurillians sending him a message—sending Earth a message? Jarka swore he would make Earth aware of the plight of color-crossers, and he intended to do so despite this little demonstration.

"Your deaths will not be in vain!" vowed Jarka as he left the communications center and made his way back to his room. "Your deaths will not be in vain," he repeated.

As the starship left orbit, Jarka looked out of his visi-port at the sphere known as Aurillia. He had come to know something of this, the first extraterrestrial community, and had learned to appreciate their culture and their beliefs. As he watched Aurillia slowly shrink, he knew he would likely not get the chance to visit this wondrous and dreaded place again in his lifetime, let alone get a chance to travel through the vast expanses of space. His attention focused on the huge volume of tapes and notes accumulated in just twenty-one days. Despite the deaths of Casla and Asdra, he grinned at the thought of the countless years it would take to study and interpret this incredible amount of information. He thought it only appropriate he write a brief conclusion of his impressions of the distant world known by its inhabitants as Aurillia.

MEMORANDUM

January 27, 2307

TO: The International Association of Exosociology
     Journal of Aurillian Studies
FR: Jarka Moosha, Ph.D.
     Mission Specialist and Principal Investigator, AE3
RE: Commentary on Aurillian Society

Individuals in Aurillian society are virtually identical in almost every way except two, the Color of their outer attire and the small ornament in the middle of their forehead. While the miracle of genetics unfolds to produce each new life, fate seems to dictate the Color each new Aurillian will wear. By Earth standards, the Color of one's clothes is trivial; meaningless for all practical purposes. And yet, in the absence of any other difference, this relatively inconsequential factor has become something monstrous on Aurillia—something that can, if disturbed, invoke nausea, arouse suspicion, and lead to death. The logical summation of this set of circumstances is that the more identical those within a society are, the less tolerant the society is of any difference. So intolerant of this difference are the Aurillians, that it is the only reason one is put to death on this otherwise crime-free and war-free planet.

Greed and lust and anger fill Aurillia's past. Their Deities—the Supreme Sree—took away those distasteful emotions from the Aurillians. Now, thousands of years later, they have been replaced with the fear of returning to the old way of life.

The welfare of the two hundred twenty-seven million individuals has been placed on one side of the sociological scales; the just demands of an uncounted group on the other. Could one say those who color-cross deserve to die? Injustice by what standards? Earth's? Aurillia's? And who are we that we should judge?

Perhaps mankind will learn something about itself by studying Aurillia. Maybe looking in this extraterrestrial mirror will show the stupidity of the artificial boundaries mankind has erected throughout the fiber of its societies. If man can observe Aurillia with open eyes, open minds, and open hearts, it is possible the often terrible consequences of having divisions will make themselves blatantly apparent. Then, GOD willing, mankind can finally let go of its need to segregate, scrutinize, and ostracize itself without fear of ever going back.

—— o0o ——

"Your beauty should not come from
outward adornment, such as braided hair and
the wearing of gold jewelry and fine clothes.
Instead, it should be that of your inner self,
the unfading beauty of a gentle and quiet spirit,
which is of great worth in GOD's sight."

I PETER 3:3-4

JOURNEY TO PRADIX

(The Seeker)

. . . .

MARION TURNED HIS HEAD around to get one last, long look at the village he had called his home for over fifty years. The late afternoon breeze caught a strand of his long silver hair, causing it to wave in front of his bearded face. The waning sunlight snuck through the break in the trees to warm his chilled cheeks.

"Good-bye, my old home—I shan't see the likes of you again," he said softly to no one but the surrounding woods. He sent a parting salute and then faced the upward slope of the narrow path once more. His hand came up to move the fallen hair back behind his ear. He leaned gently on his walking stick as he continued his relaxed pace toward the large rocky ledge up ahead—the goal for the first stint of his journey.

The ridge of the Livon Mountains ran from the barren plains of the Norther Lands to the thick forests far away in the Souther Lands. He had made this hike many times as a young lad, though not so much in recent years. As he climbed, Marion felt a mixture of emotions cross his consciousness—sadness at leaving Arvonia, so full of wonderful memories, and a joy filling his heart with the knowledge of what might lie ahead.

He halted periodically to adjust a strap on his back-pack or to take a sip of well water from his saucer-shaped canteen. He listened to the rustle of the leaves and the calls of the many birds making their homes in the treetops. He smelled the sweet aroma carried by the autumn breeze and took in the richness of the scenery and its many colors— spread out before him as if it were a prepared feast. All of this underneath a restful blue sky brought him a feeling of contentment.

As he continued his ascent, Marion began to reflect on his life, feeling and seeing everything that had ever happened to him. He relived the carefree days of his youth, roaming the hills and exploring the countryside. He thought of the walks taken with his grandfather and the countless hours asking the old man the names of trees and flowers. His grandfather's answers would always include all sorts of interesting facts about the habits of animals, the cycles of nature, and the art of living in harmony with the land.

As rich as those early memories were, none could equal the day he met Larilyn. One year later, he joined with her. Without question, it had been the happiest time of his life. He recalled the joy he felt as they took the Sacred Vows of Joining in the Central Hall. When he stood in front of his friends and family, he beamed with the knowledge that the most beautiful woman in the kingdom had agreed to join with him.

Larilyn was, indeed, a proud woman, a person full of confidence and grace. The daughter of Arvonia's only doctor, her upbringing was intellectually stimulating. And, like her father, she took an interest in all areas of healing. The only sorrow in their early lives together was their inability to have children. Soon after their joining, they realized Larilyn was barren. After their initial disappointment, they grew to accept their lot. Together they came to see each other as blessing enough and cherished one another each and every day.

He again felt the grief borne at the loss of his beloved Larilyn three years ago. His agony had been great and was only now starting to fade. Marion wondered why man must experience memories of one's life. Man was unique from the rest of the world's creatures in this ability. The process could bring much pain. Thankfully, man was given another gift—the ability to choose. Marion concluded memories are to be cherished and enjoyed. If one chooses to recount bad memories, then pain will fill one's consciousness and slowly erode one's spirit. "Relish the good and the aftertaste will linger sweetly," Larilyn wisely said before her passing. Marion was not perfect, but lately, he knew he would much rather enjoy warm thoughts about his beloved than painful ones.

While he strolled along the trail leading up the mountain, his mind continued to wander along the path of his life. After the recollection of Larilyn's passing, his memories turned to lighter fare. Marion found himself whistling as he walked. Only when evening fell and the stars came out did the need to stop and rest for the night enter his thoughts.

At the peak of the ridge defining the Livon Mountains, he found a small clearing giving him an unobstructed view of Arvonia and the Lowlands. *A prime spot to spend the night*, he thought. After a satisfying meal and a cupful of wine, Marion took out his favorite pipe. His grandfather carved it out of a deer antler many years ago. He filled it with a rich golden blend of tobacco, sat back to enjoy the aromatic smoke, and looked out across the landscape below him. He could just make out the cluster of lights from the village. It never occurred to Marion there might be so much pleasure in viewing his old home.

Glades of maples and birches framed his private panorama. The choruses of insects had not yet surrendered to the chill autumn air. Marion wondered about the purpose of their nightly serenade. There were old wives' tales telling how crickets were really kind spirits playing their songs to assist the recently departed in finding their way to the afterlife.

Marion finally allowed himself to think about his destination—Pradix. Stories about the peaceful place had been handed down from generation to generation, promising it would be filled with all the pleasures of this life, but none of its burdens. Many times he read the ancient text pledging eternal tranquility. All one needed to do was believe in its existence—and Marion did—and the path to Pradix would become clear. Marion hoped his faith in Pradix would be enough to show him the way. By leaving his heart and mind open, Marion counted on the Creator to guide him—much the way the wind carries a fallen autumn leaf to its final destination. Marion didn't know how long the journey might take. He prayed he had packed enough supplies and trusted in his own survival skills should the trip prove to be a long one. But once there, the burdens of life would vanish. He looked forward to that.

With the promise of the young man named Jhovan who first spoke of Pradix and its richness echoing through his mind, Marion felt himself slip off to a deep and satisfying sleep.

The next day was delightfully warm—quite uncharacteristic for late fall, especially at the higher altitude. Marion followed the footpath away from his campsite up toward the mountain pass. Once through the narrow gap, he quickly came upon Livon's Ledge. He stopped at the top of the sharp vertical drop. Looking out across the expanse of the prairie, he could see the majestic Meherrin Mountains off in the distance. He could even detect the winding course of the Rivanna River as it cut the tableland in half. The sight made his legs eager to start their day's work.

He turned back to the trail and began the descent off the mountain. The beauty of the day and the amazing scenery filled his mind. His thoughts then turned to which direction he would head when he reached the flatland. He halfheartedly scolded himself for not relying upon the Creator for guidance. Once he reached the plains, Marion decided to head due east. After a time, a man appeared on another path leading down from the north.

"What a fine day it is, sire. What might yer destination be, if you don't mind me askin'?" The stranger's accent reminded Marion of the folk who lived in the Wester Lands, but the smoothness of his speech made him seem special somehow.

"I'm looking for Pradix," replied Marion, not at all certain he should have admitted his intent. Some folks thought the legends about Pradix pure fantasy, the creation of the downtrodden after drinking a bit too much summer wine.

"Well, now. That's a mighty fine place to be lookin' fir, if I do say so me'self," the stranger answered while scratching his chin—contemplating the full impact of Marion's revelation.

Marion sized up the stranger and saw a compassionate face with a questioning smile and piercing eyes of some indeterminate shade of gray. He seemed quite harmless. But something about him could not be categorized. The more Marion looked, the more he realized there was little hint of his age.

"My name is Marion. And yours?" Marion finally offered.

"O'lie Peters, me name, though people often call me just plain Pete."

"Do you have any family?" Marion thought maybe that might help determine Pete's age.

"Yes, indeed. I got me a father and a—well, I guess he is sort of a brother, I'm not really sure. Anyway, I don't see 'em much on account of I'm always out travelin'," he said.

"And what do you do that causes you to travel so much?" asked Marion. He almost tacked on the phrase "for a man your age" but thought better of it.

"Oh—I travel about helping people, listenin' to their problems and doin' what I can to assist. Perhaps nudgin' them one way or another. But today, I'm headed to the Souther Lands and I thought I might cross this flatland. It is one of my favorite hikes. Make it quite often." Pete continued on after a brief pause, "But tell me more about yerself, if you don't mind me joinin' ye for a spell. Pradix, you say?"

Marion stood still for an instant, trying to determine whether Pete might believe the stories about Pradix or simply thought them fairy tales. He asked the man, "You do know of Jhovan and his journey to Pradix?"

"Oh, sure. I've heard of it," O'lie Peters said matter-of-factly. "But why don't ye tell me yer version of it. You'd be surprised how the story changes dependin' on where yer from."

"All right," Marion responded. He always did like a captive audience. The two travelers started down the path leading out to the heart of the prairie.

"Once upon a time—as bards tell it—there lived a young man in the Wester Lands named Jhovan. Evidently, there was nothing terribly special about this young man's early years. But, when he came of age, he told his father he wanted to have an adventure before he settled down.

"His father said to him, 'What in blazes do ye want to go and travel to some strange place for when ye have all the adventure ye could want right here in the Wester Lands?'

"But the young man was insistent and made plans to set off as soon as the snows of winter melted—despite his father's objection. He left the Wester Lands and journeyed east, always toward the rising sun.

"One day, Jhovan came upon a long and narrow valley full of towering trees and beautiful flowers. The sides were quite steep and periodically decorated with thin waterfalls. The east side of the valley was a sheer granite wall with only a small opening at its base. A thunderstorm suddenly appeared over the mountain. So violent was the storm and so intense was the lightning that he sought shelter within the cave. The storm did not let up but went on and on.

"Night came and a wet darkness began to fall. Jhovan realized he had no wood for a fire. Any wood he might gather near the mouth of the cave would most certainly be soaked with the day's rain. His clothes were wet and the cave was cold and damp. But as the last bit of light left the rainy sky, total blackness did not come. The perplexed young man turned toward the back of the cave and noticed a very faint glow emanating from a passageway leading deep into the mountain.

"Curiosity filled Jhovan. He got up and made his way toward the tunnel. With each step, the air in the passage became gradually warmer and more comfortable to breathe, and the dampness of the walls diminished until it was entirely gone. To his amazement, even his clothes started to feel drier.

"As he headed farther into the mountain, his eyes strained to look ahead into the passage. The strange illumination from the walls allowed him to see a set of stairs up ahead. His pace quickened as he yielded to his growing excitement until he reached the stairway. He began to climb with slow and cautious steps. The sound of distant wind chimes began to fill the passage as he moved steadily upward. The faint glow gave him enough light to pick out his footing on the smooth stones. He reached the top of the stairway and paused.

"Looking ahead, he saw an opening. It was similar in size to the mouth of the cave he entered earlier. He covered the distance to the opening quickly. His eyes took a moment to adjust to unexpected brightness. A most incredible view greeted him.

"A sea of shifting mists stretched out from below where he stood. As he looked from side to side, Jhovan saw the stone wall continue out to his left and to his right, meeting on the far side of the mist to form a large crater.

"In the middle of this sea of mist, rising out of the grayness, stood a plateau of sorts. A crystalline blue lake covered most of its surface. The lake had no apparent source, yet waterfalls fell from most of the plateau's edge down into the mist. An island covered with trees and flowers seemed to float in the center of the lake.

"He started to walk again, keeping one eye on the wondrous vista and the other on the descending path clinging to the rock face. He made his way along the wall of the mountain until the path turned out toward the island. A bridge of naturally fashioned stone led away from the rock face of the mountain. Every so often a stone pinnacle found its way up through the mist to support the archway.

"He walked across this bridge very slowly, being both careful and unable to move very quickly with such unusual sights around him. Soon, he found his way to its end and the plateau's edge. The path continued for only a short distance until it ended at what appeared to be a small wooden pier. A little boat was tied to one of the boards.

"The young man accepted the unspoken invitation of the boat. He climbed in, untied the rope, and the boat began to move away from its berth. He realized the boat contained no oar or paddle to steer the vessel but didn't seem to need one as a wistful breeze guided it. He could hear the beginnings of a soft chant.

"Soon he drew near to the island. The music grew more noticeable as many other voices and melodies joined the song. The wind blew the boat slowly until it came to rest at a dock fashioned much like the one it left minutes earlier.

"He got back to his feet and noticed a narrow trail leading through the trees and bushes. He began to feel something familiar drawing him, or perhaps someone calling him. He felt as though he was coming home after a long journey.

"After a short walk, he came to a small gate made of coarsely cut stone. He passed through the gate and entered into a garden. What he found amazed him. All the colors of the rainbow shone from every leaf on every flower and tree. The grass was greener than any field he could recall. The birds sang songs sweeter than any ever sung before.

"In a little clearing on a bench sat an old man dressed in white. His hair was gray and shimmered with silver highlights, and he had a gray beard to match. His ocean blue eyes called to Jhovan, and he responded by moving toward the peaceful figure.

"'Greetings, Jhovan. I am He who watches over the Realm of Creation. I am the pillar of all that is. I forged the world and fashioned all of the creatures of field and stream. I put the sun and the moon amongst the stars. I know what was, what is, and what will be.

"'Come and sit,' the old man gestured. 'This place is a gift to you and all mankind. I have worked long at making it. I call it Pradix.

"'You, Jhovan, and all like you, are my children. Each of you, if you merely believe, may share in this place forever.

"'But I need someone to carry word of it out into the world. That is why I brought you here. I know you and I know you will do this task. I will send another after your work in the world is complete. This other will help mankind and remind them of this place.'

"Jhovan was quite taken by this Creator, his Pradix, and the request made of him.

"The Creator continued. 'When you leave this place, your course will become clear and you will tell the world of this gift I give. One day, you will return and live here long past what your days in the world would have been otherwise.'

"The graceful figure rose from the bench and lifted

his right hand toward Jhovan. He touched him softly on the forehead.

"'So it is done.' The Creator sat down again.

"Jhovan awoke beneath an old tree and felt the warmth of the first brilliant rays of the morning sun. He saw the world as if for the first time, his love for life rekindled. As he stood up, he slowly turned his head to look out from the hilltop to see fields of rolling green in all directions. Just above the western horizon shone a white point of light beckoning him. A cool wind blew at the white clouds as Jhovan walked down the path from the old tree and headed to his home in the Wester Lands.

"Upon his return, Jhovan told everyone about what had happened to him. There were those who disbelieved him and there were those who thought he was outright crazy. But Jhovan was not daunted. He took his charge from the Creator of Pradix to heart and left his home to spread the word of Pradix and the blessings awaiting all who will believe. There were many towns that disliked Jhovan and claimed his message to be rubbish. No one is quite certain what eventually happened to Jhovan. Some think he was killed, some think he died, and still others think he awaits the believers at Pradix.

"There have been many who set out with the intent of finding Pradix and returning to confirm or deny its existence, but none have ever come back. Legend has it that Jhovan left a Gatekeeper behind to help those seeking Pradix. No one seems to know who this person is or how he has lived hundreds of years since the time of Jhovan."

"That's quite a story," remarked the old traveler. "Do you believe any of it?"

"I do. I wouldn't be here now if I didn't."

"Why?"

Marion turned to look at O'lie Peters.

"I believe it because it touches something deep down inside me. I want to believe there is something bigger and grander, that we were created not just to spend a few years in this world, but to be more."

After Marion finished his story, they realized they had walked a very long way, saw it was midday, and decided to stop for a rest and a bite of lunch. They found a comfortable grassy spot underneath a shade tree beside a stream running down a gentle slope to the Rivanna River—just out of sight.

After lunch, they started off again to follow the course of the stream to the western shore of the great river. Taking off their sweat-stained clothes and bundling them together with their other possessions, they waded into the shallow part of the river. At midstream, the cool water reached their shoulders. Once across the river, the warmth of the sun helped to dry them as they made preparations to start off once more.

They continued to walk through the tall grasses. Up gentle slopes and down rolling hills they went, knowing there was still a long way to go before they reached Meherrin Pass. The afternoon sun grew hot on the tops of their heads. Every once in a while they would stop and rest. When hungry or thirsty, they snacked on some of Marion's provisions or drank a little of the cool water collected at the river.

As they walked along, they shared stretches of conversation about the surroundings or the wildlife venturing out for a look at the travelers. When talk focused on more pertinent things, Marion started to realize it was always his life they ended up discussing. The more time Marion spent with this stranger and the more they talked, the less he learned about his companion. Unsettling as this was, Marion did not seem to be having much luck at turning the conversation around.

In the middle of the afternoon, they came up over a low-lying ridge and noticed the proud peaks of the Meherrin Mountains rising up in front of them. Marion looked at the position of the westering sun in the still-blue sky and figured they could make it to the pass before total darkness descended upon them. After a brief stop to take in the view, they set off at a brisker pace, just in case.

Approaching the mountain pass several hours later, O'lie Peters announced he wanted to continue his walk despite the gathering darkness. Marion surprised himself by urging him to stop and rest.

"It is almost dark and you won't be able to find your way. And I'm happy to share my food with you," offered Marion. "Come on—help me gather up wood for a fire."

After collecting a sufficient supply of kindling and branches, O'lie Peters watched Marion pull food and camping equipment out of his leather pack. "You know," explained Marion, "I only packed enough provisions to last me for a week or so. I'm not sure now why I didn't bring more, but—somehow—it didn't seem to matter. I suppose I decided that if Pradix was everything it was said to be, I would find it in a reasonable amount of time, and food would either be provided or it simply wouldn't be needed. I guess it's just an example of my faith in Jhovan's story and the existence of Pradix."

Marion started a fire and placed food over the burning wood. The evening soon closed in over the traveling companions. The sun dipped below the tips of the majestic trees and the stillness of the forest seemed more noticeable than ever. Almost in response to the quiet dusk, a choir of crickets sought to cheer up all creatures within earshot with their whimsical melodies.

The travelers shared a meal of hearty bread and cheese, dried fruits, and roasted meat followed by sweet Arvonian wine. After they finished, Marion watched the stars turn on one by one. At their feet, the logs in the small fire slowly melted into reddish embers. The two said nothing to another for a long while. Before drowsiness claimed Marion, he directed one more question to O'lie Peters.

"You seem a person full of wisdom. What do your instincts tell you about the truth behind Pradix?" asked Marion.

"I think what is important here is what ye believe to be the truth. Do ye truly believe in Pradix?" he murmured softly, more making a statement of fact than asking a question. "Just think what life would be like if the world knew without any doubt that Pradix really existed, and everyone knew how to find their way to Pradix in his or her own time. True—we would not have to go through life carrying 'round the fear of death. But what would life become? Would each of us stop trying to grow, learn, or build? Life might even seem futile if we knew the absolute truth. Perhaps it is better for each of us if the splendors of Pradix are not so easily revealed. Yes?"

Marion looked up at him. The red glow of the embers painted a mask of interesting hollows and angular lines on the stranger's face—a face hiding more knowledge than Marion could imagine.

"No, you are right," Marion replied. "I'm not sure man could handle such certainty about the existence of Pradix."

In the fire's dying light, Pete took on a much older appearance as he stared at the coals as though seeing another time and place. Marion got up to get a few more sticks of wood and nursed the fire back to life. As the flames took hold, the other man straightened, and a look of confidence slowly crept across his face. The inscrutable eyes of the seemingly older man widened as he leaned forward to speak with Marion face-to-face, eye-to-eye. "You have followed your own path and have believed in what you've done."

After a few minutes of listening to the crackling of the fire, Marion said, "In the morning, then." Almost as an afterthought, Marion inquired of O'lie Peters, "By the way, how old are you?"

But his traveling companion, succumbing to sleep, only mumbled in response, "In the morning, then." With those words, the conversation ended for the day.

The next morning when Marion awoke, his companion and his sleeping roll were gone. Marion hadn't noticed before that O'lie Peters didn't travel with many supplies, things one would normally have if they were going on a long trip. But instead of concern for his newfound friend's disappearance, Marion's mind opened up, as if set free from some cloud. He wanted to begin his day's travel. Maybe Pete had gone on ahead, thought Marion as he packed up his cooking utensils and rolled up his blanket, fastening it to the bottom of his backpack. He started off in the direction of Gilbert's Ledge, thinking he might catch up with Pete—if that was, in fact, where he was headed.

After hiking along the ridge of the Meherrin Mountains

for an hour or so, Marion veered off the main trail and came to the high point of the ledge. This particular vantage point always impressed him. But what greeted Marion's eyes was not the vista he expected. Instead of seeing the Great Plains beyond, he saw a long valley, full of delicate threads of mist weaving their way through countless tall trees. Down from several unseen sources in the high stone peaks crowning the valley fell slender cascades of water. He looked across the valley and saw a sheer rock face at the far end.

"Wait a minute! What happened to the plains? Why have I never seen this before? Surely I am not lost," Marion mumbled to himself in disbelief. Then a thought shot through him like a bolt of lightning. "A valley with a sheer rock face at one end? Could this be the entrance into Pradix?" he asked himself aloud. He quickly forgot about trying to find O'lie Peters and decided to strike off toward the valley. "What if I have found what I am looking for?" he said excitedly.

Marion descended from the ledge toward the valley. The path zigzagged its way down the steep slope through a deeply shaded forest. The switchbacks helped make the descent more gradual. As he walked, Marion began to think about whether there existed a Gatekeeper. Perhaps some bard added the fanciful augmentation to the legend hundreds of years ago. Why would anyone choose to live out here? Most certainly it was beautiful, but since a Gatekeeper can't live forever, from where did new Gatekeepers come? Who chose them? Who trained them? Marion had answers for none of these questions.

Several hours later Marion reached the eastern end of the valley and stood facing the sheer granite wall. He noticed a flat area in the center of the stone formation. Moss and salt deposits from years of mineral-laden water trickling over it covered its surface. As he stepped up to the rock to get a closer look, he realized there were letters carved into the stone. The workmanship was not of high quality, appearing to have been done by someone who was not experienced or in a hurry—or both. Marion began to wonder if it was the handiwork of Jhovan himself.

As he read the words, he shouted out, "That's it! The Gatekeeper isn't a person at all!" The Gatekeeper was but a rock wall engraved with one simple question. The question was this—"Do you believe?"

"Yes," sighed a world-weary Marion. "Yes, most definitely."

To the right of the Gatekeeper's question was an entrance to a cave. Marion stepped into the opening, slowly at first because he was unsure of the texture of the cave's floor and his eyes had yet to adjust to the absence of sunlight. But he found the rock surface to be smooth, almost like the glaze one might find on a piece of fine pottery.

After his eyes adjusted to the dark, he started down the long passageway. His pace picked up with each new step. Marion became keenly aware of his environment. He could feel a warm breeze where one might expect cool air. He assumed it would become darker as he moved farther into the tunnel, but it did not. With each footfall, Marion felt as though the weight of his years were falling to the floor—that he was lighter somehow. Rejuvenated. Reenergized.

Marion found the winding spiral staircase at the end of the tunnel's long entrance—just as the stories told. He set his foot on the lowest step. The wide stairway appeared sound and undamaged despite the fact it must be hundreds, maybe thousands, of years old. With renewed confidence, Marion pressed on ahead up the great steps. A faint radiance grew in intensity.

At the top of the ancient steps, a circle of light marked the other end of the tunnel. As he approached the opening, a newfound joy filled his heart and spilled over into every corner of his mind and body. The light became brighter and brighter with each step. Unlike the sun though, it was a brightness that didn't hurt his eyes.

Then Marion saw it—Pradix, in all of its splendor, opening up before him. It was just as Jhovan promised! The sunshine above, the sea of mist below, and the island surrounded by its waterfalls. Marion took a moment to gaze out at the wondrous view before he continued down the pathway to his right. He hugged the rock face and followed the narrow trail to the stone bridge, then headed out over the mists to the island.

At the end of the path, he stopped quite abruptly and stared in disbelief. There stood the forms of two men and a woman, all surrounded by shimmering light. The woman he recognized instantly—as he did the first man—but not the second man. Then it struck him. Of course! The second man fit the descriptions in the stories of old perfectly.

"Larilyn! O'lie Peters! Jhovan?"

—— o0o ——

"Then their eyes were opened and they recognized him."
LUKE 24:31

OLD MIMS

(The Savior)

. . . .

"WHAT IS GOING THROUGH THAT withered brain of yours tonight, Old Mims?" reprimanded Ormon as he came around the corner of Mims's front porch. "I would think you'd have better things to do than to sit in that old rocker staring out at the drab sky."

"I'm watching the sunset. I'm thinking about writing another story," said Mims.

"You've been an author all of your life. What can you possibly say about a sunset you haven't already said a thousand times?" Ormon laughed. "You spend far too much time alone in that broken-down house behind your type-writer! And for what? You've made all the money you're ever going to make."

"Don't start with me tonight, Ormon. I appreciate your concern, but it shan't change the way I live my life." Mims rose to greet his longtime neighbor. "What brings you up the road this far? And don't tell me you're just checking up on me."

"You know, Old Mims," Ormon started out, "you and I have more in common than either of us might care to admit. We are both living out our remaining days. We're both alone and we don't have much to look forward to. Frankly, I've been thinking about this state of affairs and, well, I just can't stand the thought of waiting around for the end. Day after day after day—the same old thing."

"You're just obsessed, Ormon. You have nothing to occupy your mind. Why do you think I write so much? It takes my mind off the drudgery." Mims smiled to himself in a sort of satisfying way.

"And what do you write about again?" asked Ormon, almost in a serious tone.

"Ormon, my poor dear friend. You know I write about life and how each of us sees it from a different perspective—through a different set of eyes. I allow myself to imagine what it might be like to live life in someone else's shoes. Sometimes the shoes are covered with rhinestones, sometimes the shoes are worn out with holes in the bottom. But people, no matter where they are in life, have dreams and they have their own private little tragedies. There is so much to explore—so much potential within each of us.

"But you already know that—you've read my stories," continued Mims, "and you know we all dream and some of us push our dreams out into reality where they can collide or collude with, complement, corrupt, or obliterate the natural order of things."

"Yes, yes—I do know all of that," replied Ormon. "You examine the dreams of your characters with the precision of a skilled surgeon. And you claim dreams are incredible gifts given to us. But to help us through times of despair and to tempt us with what could be? I don't know. You wade through the depths of your characters' collective pain with equal dexterity. You open them to the elements and expose them to the emotional vultures.

"And you're right—I've read all of your books and their pages are full of the wreckage of the twisted lives you create. I think you must take some type of perverse pleasure in birthing these defenseless creatures, invading their dreams, and causing them unending pain and hardship. Instead of facing the bleak solitude of your final days by yourself and your own emotions, you sit around and dream up characters upon whom you dump the agony you refuse to accept for yourself. Some pastime you got going on there, Old Mims."

"You know, if I didn't know better, I'd say you're trying damn hard to—how did you say it—'dump the agony *you* refuse to accept for *your*self' onto me!" Mims leaned back in his rocking chair and pushed off with his feet to start the chair squeaking back and forth. After an uncomfortable pause, Mims continued. "You might criticize my approach, Ormon, but at least when the torment of another day's monotony reaches into my soul and nags at the yearnings there, I have a place to go—something to do, somewhere to put my heartache. Once it's on the paper, it just doesn't seem to bother me anymore. And if it makes me feel better, who the hell cares?"

"You still can't convince me your bleeding all over typing paper is good for the soul. What I can't figure out is from where do these wretched individuals you dream up come? Is there some repository of dark characters in the back of your mind you tap into every time you write one of your stories? Have you ever thought maybe someone 'upstairs' is dropping these folks into your pitiful little brain because He can't bear the thought of giving them life any other way? What if a power greater than you or me is pulling all of the strings in this grand ol' universe and there really isn't any such thing as individual creativity?"

A night fly buzzed about Mims's gray hair. "I hate to burst your philosophic bubble, but you haven't said anything that hasn't been thought about or written before."

"Eh—a lot of gratitude I get! An old man walks half a mile up the road to check in on an old friend and for what? Nothing but a bunch of backtalk. I think I'll take my leave now. Maybe that dusty bottle of whiskey down the road will keep me company again tonight." Ormon got up and made his way down the uneven steps. "Good night, Old Mims."

"If you must, Ormon. Take care of yourself."

Mims watched the darkness envelop Ormon's retreating figure as he walked down the lane. Mims thought he noticed a hint of a limp in Ormon's step, not something a younger Mims might notice, but it did seem to be there. Mims felt sorry for him. Whereas Ormon had been married for many long years and known the pleasures of a wonderful loving wife, Mims had only known his writing. Now that Ormon's wife had passed, there was a raw blister in Ormon's heart that never healed. But Mims still had his lifelong love—writing. *My companion will be with me until the end*, thought the aging author. *No heartache for me. Poor Ormon.*

Mims headed for the inside of his comfortable little home. After placing the latch on the front door, he performed his nightly ritual of walking around turning off all of the lights. While his fingers searched for the switches hidden underneath the hot bulbs, he started thinking about what his graying friend said.

"There is a kernel of truth in Ormon's words, though. Maybe I am able to face the hard times in life by creating characters and having them live the dreams and bear the pains that I cannot." He stopped in mid-step to contemplate, then continued on his journey through the darkening innards of the house. "But this stuff Ormon brings up about there being some greater power planting characters in my mind for me to discover and use in my work—where does he come up with these ideas anyway?"

Mims reached his bedroom, disrobed, and headed into the bathroom to brush his teeth and wash his face. He returned to the bedroom and lifted his now tired body onto the mattress several feet off the hardwood floor.

"Sleep, my good friend! Come and take me," he whispered. Off Mims's mind set for the land of slumber. His consciousness dropped gently down through layers of undefined internal mists until he awoke within the confines of a dream.

He stood in the middle of a large field. He didn't find it particularly peaceful and noted the sparse ground covering beneath him and the pale gray sky above him. Then, one by one, figures began to approach him. As they got closer, he could recognize them despite their shifting and often incomplete bodies. He recognized them as characters from the stories, articles, and books he had authored during the course of his career as a writer. As each one approached, Mims noticed their eyes—so often full of sadness and tears. He could hear the quiet cries brought on by the memories of their burdens. He could see the pain within their hearts. It seemed as though he could peer right through their ghostly chests and read the stories of their misfortunes, stories he knew all too well because he had written them.

"Oh, my GOD," he said to himself. "Look what I've done to these poor folk." Mims surprised himself as he remembered he was in a dream and these people didn't exist—they weren't real! They were products of his own mind, yes, but they lived only within the pages of books. He couldn't get over the way they all just stood there looking at him—so pitiful. Then he woke up in a cold sweat.

"It was just a dream," he told himself without much success. His mind relived the script of the strange dream over and over again. He tried to go back to sleep, but the chorus of crickets outside his partially opened bedroom window seemed to get louder as his frustration over not being able to fall asleep mounted. He tried to turn his thoughts to the story idea that popped into his mind the previous afternoon. The storyline focused on a young man wrongly accused of being responsible for the death of a young girl. Mims thought the reading public to be overly fascinated with these sorts of stories of late. He struggled for ways to make the plot stand out, to say something about the social fabric of the day in which countless innocent people are falsely accused of things and forced to bear the ramifications because of an inability to combat the system. Mims contemplated highlighting the devotion of the young man's lover, even in the face of adversity. The man would eventually lose everything except his lover, and they would set off to rebuild their shattered lives in the end.

Mims finally decided to get out of bed and put some of his thoughts on paper or he would never go back to sleep. As he placed the first sheet of blank paper into the typewriter, he stopped suddenly. "What am I doing? I am doing it again, aren't I? I am creating yet another poor pathetic character who must endure some sort of endless suffering. Why am I doing this?" Mims remembered the faces of the characters in his dream. He took the paper out of the machine and turned off the light in his office. He sat in the darkness for several long minutes.

"Great!" Mims said to himself. "I can't sleep and I can't write. What am I supposed to do now?" As he sat for what seemed a long time, he slowly felt the grip of sleep encroaching on his mind. Pieces of thoughts started bumping into one another and rearranging themselves. New ideas coalesced from seemingly unrelated building blocks. Despite his increasing weariness, Mims could sense the creative process taking place and allowed it to continue without interference.

Then, in his writer's imagination, he started to wonder if this place he had visited in his dream might represent a sort of heaven to which characters, at least *his* characters anyway, went after their story lives were complete.

He considered the traits his characters seemed to share. He realized the misfortunes befallen the children of his imagination originated from their lack of self-respect, or their failure to accept responsibility for their own lives, or anger they wrongfully assigned to others. It all boiled down to a lack of love for themselves—perhaps this being why his characters found it so hard to love others and so often lamented their unfulfilled dreams. "No wonder they appeared to be in so much pain," Mims mumbled as he came to these conclusions. "It is one thing to create another individual in your head and put them on paper. It is another thing altogether to meet them face-to-face."

He thought about his plan for the man in his latest, as

134

of yet unwritten, story. His plight would be the opposite of those faced by his previous characters. This new character would be innocent and decent. What would happen to him would be the result of the misguided beliefs of others and their desire to lash out, to blame someone else, anybody else, for their own hardships. Mims then took it one step further and wondered what it might be like to concoct a character who takes on the anger, the pain, and the worst that man can offer up out of choice—perhaps even out of love.

Slowly, the process of working out the intricacies of this new theme switched back on his conscious mind. "What if I created this character? Perhaps he might find his way to the nether world of my dream, take on the trials of those already there, and free them from their pitiful eternal life.

"What am I thinking?" Mims clenched his fist and banged his desktop. He then noticed he was still sitting in the dark in his office at his desk. He reached for the light, clicked it on, put paper back in his typewriter, and wrote with abandon until the sun stretched its waking arms above the horizon.

Six hours passed. Mims stopped to give his tired mind and aching back a break. He rose from his chair, eyes wide from lack of sleep, and headed for the kitchen. The angle of the sunlight coming through the window above the sink told him it was midmorning already. The rumbling in his stomach reminded him it was way past time for something to eat.

After the difficult night, he found some comfort in the routine of fixing breakfast. A creature of habit, Mims usually fixed the same thing for breakfast every day. He usually ate the same thing for lunch every day. Others might think this boring, but Mims preferred not having to make any more decisions in his day than necessary. Only at dinner did he get creative and fix different dishes. He made a hot cup of strong coffee and sat down to enjoy the singing of the birds while he waited for his oatmeal to cook.

After he drained the last of the coffee from his mug, he placed the dirty dishes into the sink and went to the bedroom to find some work clothes. Yes—some time in his garden might ease his mind and body. The tomatoes and early corn needed weeding. The makeshift scarecrow needed straightening.

As he reached the cucumbers, a familiar voice startled him. "Good morning, Old Mims," said Ormon.

"Don't you know better than to scare me like that? Are you trying to do in the last remaining person on this planet who will talk to you?" said Mims, agitated.

"Eh—calm down. No harm done."

"Well, now that you've interrupted my gardening, why don't you go around to the porch. I'll meet you there with two lemonades," offered Mims as he removed his stained work gloves. "I could use a break right about now."

The men rendezvoused on the front porch and settled themselves into their usual chairs. "You know, Ormon, you have a way of making words stick. That spiel last night about someone 'upstairs' dropping characters into my mind for me to use as I please and the painful existence I create for them—you really outdid yourself this time—"

"Finally listening to reason, are you?" Ormon interjected, not being one to miss a chance to score a point.

"I want to tell you about a dream I had last night,"

continued Mims. He paused to compose himself, then relayed the dream with all of its graphic details to his neighbor. Ormon raised his glass to his lips occasionally and sipped his lemonade while Mims spoke. Once Mims finished, he closed his eyes. They sat in silence.

Then Mims eyes snapped open. "You're thinking about something, aren't you?"

"I'm thinking that's quite an interesting twist," Ormon responded. "I started off contemplating where these pitiful characters come from and you wind up with a dream about where they go after you're done with them. An almost equally bizarre concept, if I do say so myself."

"Oh, but Ormon—if you could only have seen their faces. They kept acting as if they wanted something from me and I don't know what it is. Furthermore, I'm not sure why I even care. I can't figure it out."

"Well, my friend," said Ormon as he finished the last of his lemonade. "You just keep that prized imagination of yours fired up and I'm sure you'll figure something out. I've got to run now—got a hot date with the hardware store. Oh, and one other thing—you know I hate it when you leave the pulp in my lemonade!"

"Huh? Oh, sorry. I forgot," apologized Mims. "Thanks for stopping by, Ormon. I really did need to talk."

Ormon got in his rusted-out pickup truck, turned around, and headed off down the road in a cloud of dust. Mims felt tired, went in from the porch, and lay down on the faded sofa in the living room. He shut his eyes and he soon fell fast asleep.

Before long, he found himself in the same landscape as his earlier dream. When he realized this, he experienced a sinking feeling. He didn't want to be in this place again!

Then, as before, figures came toward him. He knew their faces and silently named each as they passed him on their way to form a large circle around him. He heard their cries and felt the pain in their hearts.

"What do you want from me?" he finally shouted at them. Several minutes passed without any response.

By now his guilt spilled over his emotional dam. Mims could not contain it any longer. "I'm sorry I did this to you. I didn't know there was such a place as this. I didn't realize that when I wrote, I was actually giving you life. How can I help you? I am not a cruel person at heart. I was just making a living. Please answer me!"

In the inner ears of his mind, he heard something—not a single voice, but rather a chorus of voices, as if they were all speaking at once. The agony Mims sensed earlier filled the chorus.

"You created us. You gave us life. You did not completely define us. Our forms are as they are because you described only those parts of us serving your story. We want to be complete. We want resolution for our respective tragedies. We want our loves back. We want our lives back as they were before you found us. We want peace."

Mims stood frozen in place, asking no further questions. He didn't know what to say or how to help. The chorus continued.

"Unless you help us, your fate will be to join us in our misery—for all eternity. Once you are gone, you can't ever rectify the situation. You must help us now, while there is still time."

Then the chorus spoke no more. There was only the persistent stare from the incomplete eyes of his characters. Mims felt like a pin cushion, their stares acting as sharp metal objects being pushed, even hammered, into his aching body.

"Stop it!" he screamed at their unhearing ears. "Stop staring at me like that! My stories did not hurt anyone!"

Mims awoke with a start. Sweat covered his forehead and his upper lip. He sat up and noticed the pattern of sunlight on the opposite wall. *Late afternoon*, he thought. *What do I do now?*

Mims waited for evening before returning to his desk. He wanted his thoughts to clear. He knew he must do something, if for no other reason than to avoid having the dream again. He didn't know how many more times he could handle it.

So, in his usual manner of dealing with the problems in his life, he started writing. He decided to create one last character. Someone different from all of his previous characters. He allowed his mind to roam back to a thought from the middle of the night and to his early morning writing. What would it be like to devise a character who felt only love—not pain, not anger, not sadness—and could give only love.

"If the characters I create somehow find their way to the afterlife I experienced in my dream," Mims said to himself, "then this character will find his way there, too. The only thing I can think of to do for my children is to send them someone who will love them and take their pains on as his own."

Mims started writing. The metal letters of the typewriter flew against the paper at an incredible pace. He wrote the narrative as swiftly as he could because he didn't know how much time, how much living, remained for him. The words "while there is still time" echoed in his mind. That is what the characters in the dream said. Page after page filled with the story of a man who was born—no, brought—into the world to love mankind, no matter who they were or what their lives were like.

Will I make it until tomorrow? Mims thought as his fingers pounded out line after line. *Maybe. Will I make it until the end of the week? Doubtful.* He felt a terrible sense of impending doom, as though the certainty of a deadline on his life now drove the hasty narration to completion.

Mims finally sat back in his chair as the ship's clock on the fireplace mantle chimed eight times—midnight. The draft finished, he reached for the first page and began to proofread his latest creation. After an hour of adjusting words here and fixing a phrase there, he set about retyping the story. Sleep no longer mattered. He must finish this work before he could rest.

The clock sounded six bells—three o'clock in the morning. Mims's tired fingers stopped; the typewriter fell silent. He neatly stacked the pages of his freshly minted story, slid a paper clip down over the manuscript, and placed it into a heavy manila envelope. His publisher had been prodding him for something, anything, of late. He hoped his short story would be appreciated, and for the sake of his deceased characters, published. He scrawled the address onto the center of the envelope, licked the backs of the proper number of stamps, and pressed them onto the corner. He placed the manuscript on the edge of his desk and retired to his bedroom. Without so much as bothering to remove his clothes or brush his teeth, he climbed onto the quilt-covered bed.

He lay stiffly on his back and the minutes passed, and then the quarter hours. His neck hurt. He kept going through his story to make certain he hadn't missed anything. Once convinced everything was just right, he finally fell into an uneasy sleep.

For a third time Mims found himself in the now familiar setting, the ground still sparsely covered and the sky still tinted gray. This time something was different, though. As he noticed his surroundings, he found himself wearing a white robe—floor length with a white cord wrapped around his waist.

He looked up as he heard the rustle of moving feet across the dried leaves and grasses lying upon the dreamscape. His characters approached him again. As they moved closer, the sky behind them began to turn a brilliant blue, and the ground became blanketed with lush green grass. Old Mims immediately realized that his two previous dreams had been in black and white. The characters slowly started to change, too. Their clothes took on various colors and patterns. Their forms now complete, each having full faces and bodies. Most notably, they all smiled.

Instead of passing by Mims on their way to the circle with only a glance, each stopped this time, directly in front of Mims. Each one reached out to embrace their Creator. As Mims extended his arms in response to embrace the first character, he didn't expect there would be any substance. But to his surprise, the character's form felt complete—flesh and blood. Mims gave a warm squeeze to each, and as he did so, he felt love for the children of his imagination.

After Mims embraced the last of them, every fragment of the dreamscape was full of radiant color. His creations surrounded him. Everything seemed right. He felt a tremendous sense of satisfaction and relished it.

One of the characters broke the silence. "We thank you, Creator. We thank you for completeness, we thank you for love. Most of all, we thank you for the gift of yourself.

"Welcome."

—— o0o ——

"Who gave himself for us, that he might redeem us
from all iniquity, and purify unto himself
a peculiar people, zealous of good works."
TITUS 2:14

EPILOGUE

(The Spirit)

. . . .

I TURNED TO LOOK BACK at the planet on which I just spent the last eighty-plus years. It was as if I was a silent diver slowly coming up for air after exploring a ridge of coral, full of schools of welcoming fish. The sea was blue-green and shafts of sunlight penetrated down from an unseen sun above. All of my life my spirit cried out for this water, begging GOD to grant me the meaning of life and the memory of His love.

The salt from the tropical waters surrounding me now became the stars in a cosmic ocean. The camouflage covering me during my earthly days now lifted. And the spirits are now greeting me and returning to me the meaning of love and the memory of GOD.

little tornadoes
(in memory of holly)

we are like little tornadoes.
   we drop down from the clouds
      find the earth with our toes,
    wander about without knowing where—
our paths dispense their destruction
    without meaning to hurt
      what we touch.
    and when we are done,
we are sucked back up
   into the heavens—
      what becomes of us?

there will be other tornadoes
   on other days
      but they will not be us.

july 26, 2004
the bodhi tree house

ABOUT THE AUTHOR

NANCY JOIE WILKIE worked for over thirty years in both the biotechnology industry and as part of the federal government's biodefense effort. She served as a project manager, providing oversight for the development of many new products.

Now retired, she composes original music, plays a variety of instruments, and is currently recording many of her compositions. She also created a series of original greeting cards that display her artwork and photographs. Her cards and prints have been sighted at various charity events.

Seven Sides of Self is her first publication of fiction. She is currently working on a novella, a science fiction novel, and more short stories—including a children's story.

She resides in Brookeville, Maryland.

Creations by Nancy Joie Wilkie

CD—*Meditations on the Day* (February 2016)

CD—*Pauper, Piper, Princes* (March 2017)

CD—*Venus in the Trees* (April 2019)

Greeting Cards and Prints by Mindsights Mediaworks

Coming Soon

CD—*Aurillian Tales* (2020)

Visit www.mindsights.net for updates on new creations.

SELECTED TITLES FROM SHE WRITES PRESS

She Writes Press is an independent publishing company founded to serve women writers everywhere. Visit us at www.shewritespress.com.

Our Love Could Light the World by Anne Leigh Parrish. $15.95, 978-1-938314-44-5. Twelve stories depicting a dysfunctional and chaotic—yet lovable—family that has to band together in order to survive.

The Afterlife of Kenzaburo Tsuruda by Elisabeth Wilkins Lombardo. $16.95, 978-1-63152-481-3. As he stumbles through an afterlife he never believed in, scientist Kenzaboro Tsuruda must make sense of his life and confront his family's secrets in order to save his ancestors from becoming Hungry Ghosts, even as his daughter, wife, and sister-in-law struggle with their own feelings of loss.

Wishful Thinking by Kamy Wicoff. $16.95, 978-1-63152-976-4. A divorced mother of two gets an app on her phone that lets her be in more than one place at the same time, and quickly goes from zero to hero in her personal and professional life—but at what cost?

The Lucidity Project by Abbey Campbell Cook. $16.95, 978-1-63152-032-7. After suffering from depression all her life, twenty-five-year-old Max Dorigan joins a mysterious research project on a Caribbean island, where she's introduced to the magical and healing world of lucid dreaming.

Time Zero by Carolyn Cohagan. $14.95, 978-1-63152-072-3. In a world where extremists have made education for girls illegal and all marriages are arranged in Manhattan, fifteen-year-old Mina Clark starts down a path of rebellion, romance, and danger that not only threatens to destroy her family's reputation but could get her killed.

The Black Velvet Coat by Jill G. Hall. $16.95, 978-1-63152-009-9. When the current owner of a black velvet coat—a San Francisco artist in search of inspiration—and the original owner, a 1960s heiress who fled her affluent life fifty years earlier, cross paths, their lives are forever changed . . . for the better.